AMERICAN CHILLERS

AMERICA'S #1 SERIES FOR MAXIMUM CHILLS!

#24: Haunting
in
New Hampshire

Johnathan Rand

An AudioCraft Publishing, Inc. book

Book storage and warehouses provided by Chillermania!©
Indian River, Michigan

Warehouse security provided by:
Lily Munster and Scooby-Boo

American Chillers #24: Haunting in New Hampshire
ISBN 13-digit: 978-1-893699-96-0

Librarians/Media Specialists:
PCIP/MARC records available **free of charge** at
www.americanchillers.com

Cover illustration by Dwayne Harris
Cover layout and design by Sue Harring

Printed in USA

HAUNTING
IN
NEW
HAMPSHIRE

VISIT CHILLERMANIA!

WORLD HEADQUARTERS FOR BOOKS BY JOHNATHAN RAND!

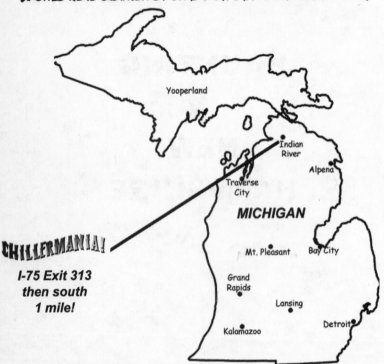

CHILLERMANIA!

*I-75 Exit 313
then south
1 mile!*

Visit the HOME for books by Johnathan Rand! Featuring books, hats, shirts, bookmarks and other cool stuff not available anywhere else in the world! Plus, watch the American Chillers website for news of special events and signings at *CHILLERMANIA!* with author Johnathan Rand! Located in northern lower Michigan, on I-75! Take exit 313 . . . then south 1 mile! For more info, call (231) 238-0338. And be afraid! Be veeeery afraaaaaaiiiid . . . .

1

If you had asked me a year ago if I believed in ghosts, I would have said, in one word:

No.

Sure, I know lots of people believe they've seen ghosts, but I'm not one of them. I like to read ghost stories, but even when I was little I was never afraid of ghosts. I used to be afraid of monsters under my bed or in my closet, but that was when I was very young. There are no monsters in closets or under the bed, just like there is no such thing as ghosts. And I wasn't afraid of them.

All that changed one horrifying summer, when

we moved into a bigger house on the other side of the city.

My name is Hannah Bayford, and I live in Concord, New Hampshire. Concord is the state capital. I have one brother named Clay. I'm twelve, and he's eight. He's a lot of fun to hang around with . . . most of the time. But he does a lot of things that gross me out. He catches frogs and puts them in his pocket. Toads, too. He used to catch worms and put them in his pocket. One time he forgot about it, and Mom found them when she was doing the laundry. She totally freaked out! It was actually pretty funny . . . but Mom got mad. Clay doesn't put worms in his pocket anymore.

We moved for a couple of reasons. Number one, Mom has always said she wanted a bigger house. And number two, Dad has always wanted to move away from the city to somewhere that wasn't so busy. I thought that would be cool. I like the forest, and I thought it would be fun to be able to wander among tall trees and build forts with my brother.

So, beginning in the spring, we started house-hunting. Every weekend, we would go for a drive and look at homes that were for sale. We looked at a lot of them. Some of them were big, but Mom and Dad said they hadn't found one that was perfect.

Until one gray, rainy, Saturday afternoon.

Looking back, I should have known something was wrong. I should have known right away that the house at the end of Cedar Mill Street wasn't what it appeared to be. Something told me right away—a little voice in my head—to stay away from the old house surrounded by huge, lofty trees.

Someone seemed to whisper in my ear:

Don't go inside. Don't go near that house.

But did I listen?

Don't go inside. Don't go near that house.

Nope. I told that little voice to go away, that it was just my imagination.

Very soon, however, I'd be wishing I'd listened to that voice. In fact, there was something that happened that very day—the day we first saw the house—that should have told all of us to stay away.

And it all started when we explored a room at the end of the hallway on the second floor of the house . . . .

We'd been driving around for about an hour. Rain had been falling most of the morning, and the roads were shiny and slick. An iron-gray sky loomed low, and a cool mist hung in the air like smoke.

Mom spotted the HOUSE FOR SALE sign first. The sign was black with orange letters: the kind you see for sale in department stores. There was a hand-drawn black arrow pointing to the right.

"There's something, right there," Mom said, and

Dad turned the car onto Cedar Mill Street. We saw several houses, but they weren't very close together. They were old and big, too . . . at least twice the size of the house we were living in. The yards were large expanses of deep green grass filled with dozens of dandelions that looked like little sunbursts. Huge trees, their gray and black trunks glossy from the rain, stood silent and still, sleeping in the morning drizzle. Rain dripped from sagging, green leaves.

"I wonder which house is for sale?" Mom said as our car crawled down the deserted street. We continued until the road came to a dead end. There, a tall, two-story house loomed behind several enormous, old trees. It seemed almost hidden behind branches and leaves.

And there was a big sign in the yard that read: FOR SALE BY OWNER.

"This is the place," Dad said, and he pulled the car into the driveway. He stopped in front of an attached two-car garage.

I looked up at the big, old house—and that's when I first heard the faint voice in my head.

Don't go inside. Don't go near that house.

Oh, I knew it was only my imagination getting

to me. The house looked a little creepy with the gray sky and the rain, but it wasn't scary looking or anything. The house was old, but it was in good shape. Someone had taken good care of it. It looked like it had a fresh coat of white paint, and the rain made it glisten. Even the black shingles on the roof seemed to shine. There was a large garden on the left side of the house, with a kaleidoscope of brilliant colors. Like the leaves of the trees, the flower petals were shiny from the rain.

"Nice place," Dad said.

"I wonder if anyone is home," Mom said.

The car idled quietly, and rain tapped on the roof and windows.

Don't go inside. Don't go near that house.

There was that voice again. Sure, I knew it was only in my head. I knew it was my own voice.

But why? We'd looked at over a dozen homes in the past couple of months. Why did I have a strange gnawing of doom in my head? What was different about this house?

Lots . . . and I was about to find out why.

"Wait here," Dad said as he opened the car door and stepped into the rain. He hustled to the covered porch and rang the doorbell.

"It sure is a big house," Clay said.

Through the rain-streaked car windows, we watched as the front door opened and a man appeared. He had gray hair and glasses. He and my dad shook hands and began talking, but we couldn't hear what they were saying. The old man nodded

19

several times, smiled, then closed the door. Dad jogged back to the car and got inside.

"His name is Mr. Hooper," he said. "He says we can come inside and take a look around." He turned the key in the ignition. The car engine died.

"We have to go out in the rain?" Clay complained.

"You're not going to melt," I said. "All we have to do is run to the front door."

I pushed the car door open and stepped out. Clay climbed out my side. Mom and Dad got out, too, and the four of us hurried to the porch. The front door opened, as if automatically. Mr. Hooper appeared again, standing aside.

"Come in, come in!" he said. "I don't get visitors very often. Come in from this rainy, cold weather!"

Upon entering, there were several things I noticed right away. We were in a big living room. The floor was made of dark brown wood, with even darker grains that looked like hair fibers. It was shiny and polished. There were several large, colorful rugs placed about, including one very big one centered in the living room. On the other side, a real fire burned real wood in a real fireplace. We have a fireplace in our home, but it burns gas and the logs are fake. All you have to do is flick a switch and *poof!* you have a fire. But *this* fire was real, and I could smell the musky odor of burnt wood. It made the room feel cozy and homey.

There was a large, fluffy black leather couch and two matching recliners. They were so big and soft they looked like they would swallow you and trap you forever. A white cat with one black ear was nestled on the arm of one of the recliners. He was sleeping, and he probably didn't even know we were there. To the left of the couch, a staircase went up to the second story. Like the floor, the steps were made of dark wood, all glossy and shiny.

I counted twelve pictures hanging from the walls. They were all portraits, and they all looked to be very old. The pictures were black and white, but several had turned a dirty yellow color over the years.

Mr. Hooper closed the door.

"That awful rain," he said as he shook his head. "It hasn't stopped since Thursday. But I hear that it's supposed to stop this morning, and we might even see a little sunshine this afternoon."

I hope so, I thought.

"Thanks for letting us take a look around your

house," Dad said. He started to take off his shoes, but the old man stopped him.

"No, no," he said. "Please. Keep your shoes on. Be comfortable. A little rain or dirt won't hurt this old house. She's seen much worse over the years. Can I bring either of you some tea?"

"That would be nice," Mom said.

"Sure," Dad said. "That sounds good on a rainy day like today."

Mr. Hooper smiled. "Good, good," he said. "Please, feel free to look around, anywhere you wish." He looked at me, then at Clay. His eyes twinkled. "And you two might want to go upstairs," he said with a widening grin. "There is a certain room at the end of the hall I think you will find very interesting." He winked, then he looked at Mom. "Be right back with your tea." He turned, walked across the living room, and vanished into the kitchen.

"Let's go upstairs," I said to Clay. I was curious about the room Mr. Hooper mentioned.

"Don't touch a single thing," Mom warned. "Remember: we're guests in this house."

"Don't worry," I said. "We won't."

Clay and I crossed the living room, walked

around the recliner and past the white cat with the black ear. He woke up and looked at me curiously. Then, he tucked his nose in his paws and closed his eyes again.

The steps creaked beneath our feet as we walked upstairs. The smell of wood smoke faded.

"I wonder how old this place is," Clay said as he climbed the steps and dragged a finger along the paneled wall.

"I don't know," I replied. "But it's *old*. Probably older than Grandpa."

At the top of the steps, a long hall opened up. Two large glass chandeliers—like swarms of glittering diamonds—burned from the ceiling. Like everything else in the home, they, too, looked very old.

There were several dark doors on either side of the hall. All were closed. The end of the hall was capped with yet another door. It, too, was closed.

Downstairs, I heard Mom and Dad talking with Mr. Hooper, but by then we were halfway down the hall, and I couldn't hear what they were saying.

And a strange thing happened as we walked toward the door at the end of the hall. A strange darkness seemed to fall over us, like a cloud slipping in front of the sun. I looked up at the glowing chandeliers, but they seemed to be just as bright as ever. The air became cooler, too, and I wondered if there was a window open somewhere.

Strange.

We reached the door at the end of the hall and stopped. The door wasn't closed all the way, and I could see a thin blade of darkness beyond the door and the frame.

The doorknob was faded brass, the color of a weathered penny. It had curious designs and patterns engraved over it. Clay reached out, but before he grasped it, he stopped suddenly.

We heard a squeak—and the door began opening . . . *all by itself!*

I was so shocked, I couldn't move. I stood at the end of the hall, watching in horror as the door slowly creaked open. Darkness poured out like ink, and a feeling of dread made my skin crawl. It felt like a million spider legs all over my body.

　　Clay had seen enough. He spun on his heels and ran, screaming, all the way down the hall like his hair was on fire. He stormed down the stairs, yelling at the top of his lungs.

But I never took my eyes off the door. It was still moving, opening slowly. Lights from the chandeliers in the hall illuminated a trunk against a wall. A window in the room also provided a murky, gray light.

There was a flurry of sounds on the stairs, like a herd of stampeding elephants. It was, of course, only Mom and Dad and Mr. Hooper. They reached the top of the stairs and rushed toward me. Clay was following them from a safe distance.

"What's wrong?!?!" Mom asked me.

I pointed. *"The door!"* I replied. *"It opened all by itself!"*

Mr. Hooper chuckled pleasantly. His eyes sparkled. "Not really," he said. "Take a few steps back."

I did as he asked.

The door began to close all by itself!

I was just as freaked out as I had been when it opened on its own . . . only now, I knew something was going on. Sure, the door was opening, but it couldn't be doing it all by itself.

"Let me show you something," Mr. Hooper said with a smile. I moved aside, and he stepped up to the door and said, "Door! I command you to open!"

The door started to open again!

Mr. Hooper took a step back.

"Door! Close!"

As soon as he spoke, the door began to close again.

He turned and looked at me. His smile was even wider. "The secret is right here," he said, and he pointed to his feet. "The floorboards are old and a little weak. When you put weight on this exact spot, it pushes the floorboards down a tiny bit. This causes the other end of the floorboards—right there at the door—to rise and put pressure on the door frame. In turn, the door opens and closes, depending on where you put your weight."

"That's cool," I said.

Clay was peering around Mom's leg. "I wasn't really afraid," he said.

I rolled my eyes. "You were screaming like you'd seen a ghost," I said.

"If you saw a ghost, you'd be screaming a lot louder than I did," Clay said.

Turns out, Clay was right—because I'd be seeing a ghost, all right . . . and it would be my turn to scream!

The five of us were still standing at the end of the hall, and Mr. Hooper spoke.

"Go ahead and take a look inside the room," he said. "It's one of my favorite places in the house. I spent lots of time in there when I was little, as have many others in my family."

He stepped toward the door. It began to open on its own, but he grabbed the knob and pushed it. Then, he reached around the wall. A light clicked on.

"And while the kids are having a look in the room," he said, glancing at Mom and Dad, "I'll show you some of the other rooms up here." He turned and walked down the hall, and Mom and Dad followed. Footsteps echoed, and Mr. Hooper began telling Mom and Dad about the house. I didn't pay attention. I was staring into the room through the doorway, mesmerized.

It was a playroom. Trees were painted on the walls, and paintings of cartoon characters were nestled within the branches. A large, smiling monkey swung from one of the branches. A colorful toucan was flying on the wall near the window. The only object in the room was a very large wooden trunk pushed against a wall, and I figured it was probably an old toy chest.

"Hey, this is cool!" Clay said, and he stepped into the room. I followed.

All four walls were colorfully painted with trees and animals. It was like stepping into a cartoon forest. Even the ceiling was painted. It was blue with a few white, puffy clouds. A yellow sun smiled down upon us. It had kind eyes and a wide grin. There were seagulls flying around it.

"Wow," I said. "This is awesome."

There were two windows on the far wall. I walked across the room and looked outside. The rain had stopped, but it was still gray and dreary. Droplets of water clung to the glass like little shiny beads.

Below, the backyard opened into a vast mesh of green lawn, as flat and smooth as a pool table. Like the front yard, there were several large trees growing. To the left was the garden, and there was another house in the distance.

And far back in the yard, I saw a black iron fence, and I drew a quick, startled breath. A tingle of nervousness trickled up my spine. The nervousness became fear, and the fear turned to horror.

But it wasn't the fence that frightened me. It was something on the other side that completely freaked me out . . . .

It was a small cemetery.

On the other side of the fence, old, gray headstones popped out of the ground like blocks of cement. There were at least twelve of them, all different sizes. Some of them were slanted. It was obvious that the headstones were very, very old.

"What's the matter?" Clay's voice surprised me, and I flinched.

I raised my arm slowly, robot-like, pointing.

"Look," I said. "Way back there."

Clay came to my side and peered out the rain-streaked window.

"That's cool!" he said. "Our very own cemetery!"

"This isn't our house," I said. "And even if Mom and Dad buy it, I'm sure the cemetery doesn't come with it."

"I bet it does," Clay said. "I bet the cemetery has a bunch of Mr. Hooper's relatives living in it."

"Don't be silly," I said with a frown. "Dead people don't *live* in a cemetery. How can they live if they're dead?"

"Doesn't matter," Clay said, shaking his head. "But this place is cool. I'll bet there are lots of great places to explore around here, including that old cemetery."

That same feeling I had when we first drove up to the house came back to me. It was a mixture of fear and dread. It was as if there was something somewhere that was trying to warn me.

This time, however, I pushed it away.

Hannah, you're being silly, I told myself. *It's just an old house. And Clay's right: there are probably a lot of really cool places to explore around here.*

34

I strode out of the playroom and went into the next bedroom. Inside, there was a single bed, a dresser, and a bookshelf filled with books. It looked like it was probably a guest room.

I heard laughter coming from a room down the hall. Dad was saying something about the house being big enough for an army. Then, I heard their footsteps enter the hall.

"You two don't get into anything," Mom called out. "We're going downstairs and into the garage."

I walked to the doorway and saw Mom, Dad, and Mr. Hooper at the end of the hall near the top of the stairs.

"We won't," I called out.

"How do you like the playroom?" Mr. Hooper asked.

"It's cool!" I said.

"Don't get into anything," Dad said as he, Mom, and Mr. Hooper started down the stairs.

I walked back into the playroom and over to the window. Then, I realized something:

Clay was gone. He was no longer in the playroom.

My brother had vanished into thin air!

"Clay?" I said.

There was no answer. I looked down the hall.

No Clay.

Where did he go? I wondered. In my mind, I calculated how long I had been in the other bedroom—maybe thirty seconds at the most. That might have been enough time for Clay to leave the playroom and go down the steps, but I'm sure I would have heard his footsteps.

Then, I figured it out. I knew *exactly* where my brother had gone and what he was up to. He was hiding behind the door. I couldn't see him, but it was the only place he could be. I was sure he was doing it just to fool me. He was probably waiting for just the right second to leap out and scare me.

So, I decided to give him the opportunity to do it. Knowing where he was and what he was up to, I wasn't afraid. In fact, maybe I could even scare *him* . . . if I was quick enough.

I turned and looked out the window, listening for any movement from behind me. I heard nothing.

He's being awfully patient, I thought. So, I decided I would get the jump on him. I would grab the door handle and pulled, exposing his hiding place. He would totally freak out!

I walked across the room, grabbed the doorknob, pulled and shouted at the same time.

"Boo!"

Clay wasn't behind the door.

That tickle of dread was coming back. I was sure there was some logical explanation as to where Clay had gone . . . but what was it? I had been in the other bedroom. Maybe he'd gone back downstairs, and

I hadn't seen him.

I hurried out of the room and down the hall, calling out my brother's name.

"Clay? Clay? Where are you? Where did you go?"

I reached the stairs and walked down the steps, still calling his name.

"Clay? *Clay?*"

I stopped at the bottom of the stairs. There were no sounds, except for the soft ticking of a clock on the fireplace mantle and the occasional pops and hisses from the fire.

"Clay?" I called out again.

The white cat was still sleeping on the recliner's armrest. He stirred, raising his head to look at me. His eyes were sleepy and blank.

"Have you seen my brother, kitty-cat?" I asked. Silly, I know. I didn't expect the cat to answer me.

But he did—sort of. The cat gave a single meow, then went back to sleep.

"I'll take that as a 'no,'" I said.

I was getting *really* worried. I had no idea where my brother was. What happened to him?

Just when I was about to call out for Mom and

Dad, I heard a noise. It sounded like a scream, but it was far away.

Then, it was louder. It was still muffled, but I recognized the voice of my brother right away.

And he was screaming, all right.

He was screaming for help!

Clay's screams sounded like they were coming from upstairs, so I turned and bounded back up the steps two at a time. Clay continued to scream, and now he was pounding on something. He sounded like he might be locked in a closet.

I ran down the hall, my footsteps echoing off the walls and ceiling. Clay's screams were coming from the playroom. By the time I reached the door, I was out of breath. Clay was still shouting and pounding.

Suddenly, it all made sense, and I knew exactly where my brother was.

I bolted across the room to the large trunk next to the wall. The trunk lid was closed, and it was latched shut. I flipped the latch and pulled up on the lid. Inside, of course, was Clay.

"What are you doing in there?" I said.

"I was hiding," he said. "You were busy looking in that other room, and I thought I would hide and jump out when you came back in here. I wanted to freak you out. But I got stuck."

Clay sat up and scrambled out of the trunk, and I examined the old brass hinge.

"When you closed the lid, the latch caught," I said. "It's a good thing I was around. You would've been trapped for a while."

"Where are Mom and Dad?" Clay asked.

"They went to look at the garage with Mr. Hooper," I replied.

"Do you think they're going to buy this place?" he asked.

I shrugged. "I don't know," I said. "But they seem to like it."

"I do, too," Clay said.

I turned and looked out the window. "Come on," I said. "It's not raining anymore. Let's go check out that old cemetery."

Clay closed the trunk lid. We left the room and walked down the hall.

"This place really is kind of cool," I said, admiring the chandeliers above.

"And big," Clay said. "It's a lot bigger than our house. This hall is like a bowling alley."

We reached the stairs and walked down. In the living room, the fire crackled and popped. The white cat remained on the armrest, sleeping soundly. The house seemed very peaceful, and I thought about how nice it would be to live here. It would be a lot of fun during the winter when we could sit by the fire and drink hot chocolate.

We strode through the living room and out the front door. The rain had stopped, but there were still droplets of water falling from the roof and dripping from the trees. The air smelled thick and fresh. Mom, Dad, and Mr. Hooper were standing in the driveway.

"Can we go into the backyard?" I asked.

Mr. Hooper waved his arm and grinned. "Sure," he said. "Feel free to look around anywhere."

"Is that your cemetery?" Clay asked.

Mr. Hooper shook his head. "No," he replied. "My property ends just before the cemetery. It's on public land. It's been there ever since I was a boy."

"Cool," Clay said.

"Don't go too far," Dad said.

We leapt off the porch and into the soft, soggy grass. Clay raced to the side of the house and disappeared around the corner. I followed, but I didn't run.

By the time I reached the side of the house, Clay was already in the backyard. He turned to see where I was.

"Hurry up, slowpoke!" he shouted. He tripped over his own foot, but he didn't fall.

I was in no hurry. As I walked along the side of the house, I marveled once again at how big it was. I hoped Mom and Dad would buy it.

Something in one of the first floor windows caught my eye, and I stopped. The glass was streaked with rain, but I could see inside. Most importantly, I could see something on the other side of the window. It was white, and I could see dark eye sockets and a gaping mouth.

The sudden realization caused every muscle in my body to tense. I gasped and almost screamed.

I knew it was impossible . . . but I was seeing it with my own eyes! I was staring at a ghost!

You're probably thinking that I started screaming my head off.

Nope.

Instead, I turned and ran back to the front of the house. Mom, Dad, and Mr. Hooper were still standing in front of the garage, talking. When they saw me, they stopped speaking.

"There's a ghost in the house!" I shouted. *"I saw a ghost through a window!"*

Mr. Hooper laughed. "A ghost, eh?" he said.

"Hannah, *really,*" Mom said.

"I'm serious!" I said. "I saw a ghost! He's in one of the rooms downstairs!"

By then, Clay had heard the commotion, and he came running from around the side of the house.

"What's going on?" he asked.

"I saw a ghost in the house!" I replied.

Clay's eyes grew wide. He didn't say anything, but I could tell he looked spooked.

"Well, then," Mr. Hooper said, "let's go have ourselves a look. Can't have a ghost wandering around, scaring everyone, can we?" He walked to the porch and into the house, followed by Mom, Dad, and Clay, then me.

"Where did you see this 'ghost?'" Mr. Hooper asked as we walked through the living room.

"I was on that side of the house, over there," I replied, pointing. "He's in one of the rooms on the first floor."

He walked to a door and pushed it open. I peered around him. The only thing I could see were shelves with tons and tons of books.

"This is my library," Mr. Hooper said. "No

ghosts in here." He closed the door. Farther down the hall was another door, and he pushed it open.

Suddenly, in the gray shadows, I saw the ghost again.

"Right there!" I said, pointing. "He's still there!"

Mr. Hooper clicked on the light. "Ah-ha!" he said. "There's your ghost!"

Suddenly, I felt very sheepish. The white form with eyes wasn't a ghost . . . but a white robe hanging on a tall bedpost. What I thought were eyes and a mouth were only places where the material had a couple of creases. From outside, through the rain-streaked window, it had only *appeared* to be a ghost.

"Rest assured," Mr. Hooper said with a laugh as he pulled the door closed. "There are no ghosts in this house. Only memories."

What a relief! I'd actually convinced myself that I'd seen a ghost in the house. Clay had, too.

And when we left that day, I knew that, if Mom and Dad decided to buy the house, I'd have nothing to worry about.

Which, of course, wasn't true. There were lots of things to worry about.

I just didn't know it, yet.

49

Well, Mom and Dad bought the house. It took another month or two, because Dad said there were lots of important papers they had to sign. He said buying a house is a big deal. It's not like going to the store and buying milk or bread.

But everything got worked out, and Mom and Dad set a moving date. I was excited, but I was a little sad. I would be leaving all my friends behind. Of course, we weren't moving very far away, and I promised everyone we would come back and visit.

Finally, moving day arrived. It was August, and the morning was sunny and bright. Some men came with a big, white truck and loaded all of our belongings into it. Dad gave them directions, and we followed them through the city to our new house.

It was strange: as we got to our new house on Cedar Mill Street, that voice spoke to me again. It was the very same voice that spoke to me the first time I saw the place.

Don't go inside. Don't go near that house.

I had completely forgotten about hearing that in my head the first time we saw the place.

Don't go inside. Don't go near that house.

Then, I remembered seeing the 'ghost' through the window on our first visit, and I laughed out loud in the back seat of our car.

Mom was in the front passenger seat, and she turned around. "What's so funny?" she asked.

"Oh, nothing," I replied with a smile. "I was just thinking about the time I thought I saw a ghost in the window, but it turned out to be Mr. Hooper's white robe."

Mom smiled. "There are no ghosts in our new

house," she said.

"I know," I replied. "Mr. Hooper said so."

Well, Mr. Hooper might have *told* us that there weren't any ghosts in the house.

But we would soon find out he was *wrong*.

11

We pulled into the driveway of our new house, right behind the big moving truck.

"We're home," Dad said, which seemed strange. It didn't feel like we were home. Maybe after we'd lived in the house for a while, it might seem like home.

And his words also stirred some recent memories. At home—our old home, that is—it had been hard to say good-bye to all my friends. They all came to our house to see us off, and I must admit, I cried a little. But I told them I would always keep in touch, and Dad reminded Clay and me that we weren't moving very far. We could visit anytime. That made me feel a little better.

We got out of the car. Dad met with the men who'd loaded and drove the big truck.

"What do we get to do?" I asked Mom. We were standing in the driveway. The morning sun warmed my face and arms. Birds were chirping in the trees. The air smelled fresh, with the faint, punky scent of a recently-mowed lawn.

"Nothing, for the time being," Mom replied. "The men have to unload all of the heavy furniture, first. After it's inside and all arranged, you can help bring in boxes and start getting your room in order. But for now, just be sure to keep away from the workers."

"Cool," Clay said. "I'm going to explore the backyard." He sprinted across the grass.

"Don't go too far," Mom called out after him.

"I won't," Clay replied, and he vanished around the side of our new home.

Dad was still talking to the workers, and he turned and called to Mom. Mom joined them at the side of the truck.

Behind me, I heard a car. I turned to see a blue pickup truck pull into our driveway. Behind the wheel was Mr. Hooper. He smiled and waved, and I waved back.

He let the truck idle as he opened the door and got out.

"Getting moved in, eh?" he said.

"Yeah," I replied. "We just got here."

"I think you'll like your new home," he said. "I sure liked it here."

"But, if you liked it here, why did you move?" I asked.

"Oh, it's just a bit too big for me anymore," he said. "And it gets a little lonely. I found a house that's a lot smaller. Nice place, and I think I'm going to like it there."

"I hope your cat likes it, too," I said.

Mr. Hooper looked at me. No . . . he *glared* at me.

"What cat?" he asked. He sounded puzzled.

"Your cat," I said. "The one I saw when we first came and looked at your house. There was a cat in the living room, sleeping on the couch by the fire."

"You must be mistaken," Mr. Hooper said, shaking his head. "I don't have a cat."

"But I saw a cat in your living room," I said. "He was sleeping, but he woke up. I saw him."

"I had a cat when I was a boy," Mr. Hooper said. "His name was Snowflake, but that was a long time ago."

Snowflake? I thought. And, although the sun warmed my skin, a sudden chill washed over me. My arms broke out in gooseflesh.

"Snowflake," I said absently. "By any chance, was Snowflake white with a black spot on one ear?"

Mr. Hooper nodded and looked at me curiously. "That's right," he replied. "But he's long gone."

"No, he's not," I insisted. "I saw him in your living room when we came to look at your house."

"I'm sorry," Mr. Hooper said as he shook his head, "but you must be mistaken. Snowflake died over fifty years ago."

12

Dad saw me talking with Mr. Hooper in the driveway, and he came over.

"Just wanted to see the place one last time," Mr. Hooper told my dad as they shook hands.

"Well, you can drop by anytime you like," Dad said.

"I might just do that," Mr. Hooper said. "You folks getting all moved in?"

"We just got here," Dad replied. "We'll get

everything unloaded today, but it will take a few days to settle in."

"I'm going to find Clay," I said. I looked at Mr. Hooper and waved. "See you later."

Mr. Hooper nodded and smiled, and I turned and walked away.

His cat died over fifty years ago? I thought as I walked through the front yard. *But that's impossible! Unless, of course, the cat I saw wasn't Snowflake. But Mr. Hooper said he didn't have a cat. Not since Snowflake.*

What on earth was going on? Whose cat did I see?

One thing I knew: Mom and Dad were in the living room when I saw the cat. So was Clay. If Clay saw the cat, that would prove I wasn't going crazy.

I walked around to the side of the house and saw Clay, far off. He was walking slowly through the cemetery, looking at the headstones.

"Clay!" I shouted, but he was too far away to hear me.

I continued walking next to the house. I looked up, shook my head, and grinned when I saw the window where I'd thought I saw a ghost. Now, it seemed so silly.

"Clay!" I called out again, but he was still too far away, and he didn't respond or even look in my direction.

By now, I was in the backyard, and our new house was behind me. As I walked past the garden through the thick, soft grass and looked around, I knew I was going to like it here. Sure, I was going to miss my old home and my friends . . . but I would make new ones, I was sure.

I reached the old cemetery, but there was no sign of Clay. There were a few big trees around, and I figured he had gone behind one of them.

"Clay!" I shouted again.

"What?" he replied . . . and I about jumped out of my skin.

It was impossible . . . but he was right behind me!

"How . . . how did you get there?!?!" I stammered.

"Get where?" Clay answered absently.

"Right there! Behind me!"

Clay shrugged. "I walked here," he said as he turned and pointed to our new home in the distance. "I was over on the other side of the house. I found a cool old tree that'll be great for climbing."

I was bewildered. "But . . . but I saw you in the cemetery," I said. "I called out to you, but you didn't hear me."

"You're right," he replied. "I didn't hear you. Like I said: I was on the other side of the house."

I gazed around the cemetery. It was the first time I had the chance to see it up close. On our first trip here, I had intended to come and check it out . . . but I wound up getting frightened by the robe in the window.

I counted thirteen gravestones. All of them were gray and weathered, and I was sure they'd been here for a long, long time.

If it wasn't Clay, then just who did I see here? I thought. *I saw someone, about the same size and height as Clay. He even looked like he was wearing the same clothes.*

I looked all around, but saw no one.

"Dad is going to have fun mowing our lawn," Clay said. "The yard is huge. It'll take him the whole weekend."

I changed the subject. "Clay," I said, "do you remember the first time we came to this house?"

Clay looked at me. "Sure," he said. "It was cold and rainy."

"Do you remember when we first went into the

living room?"

Clay gave me a strange look. "Of course I do," he said. "It was only a couple months ago. I don't forget things very fast."

"How about the white cat on the couch?" I said.

Clay frowned, and his brow knotted. "What white cat?" he asked.

"The white one with one black ear," I said. "He was sleeping on the couch near the fireplace."

"I didn't see any cat," Clay said as he shook his head.

That gnawing, fearful feeling came back. My skin tingled, and I felt chilled.

I saw a cat there, I thought. *I know it was there.*

"Forget about it," Clay said. "Come on. You've got to see that cool old tree."

Clay began walking, and I followed. But I couldn't think about the tree. All I could think about was the white cat I'd seen on the couch.

Snowflake died over fifty years ago, Mr. Hooper had said.

Fifty years ago.

Clay said he didn't see the cat—but he had walked right by the sleeping animal! How did he miss

65

it?

And just moments ago, I'd seen *someone* in the old cemetery. It might not have been my brother . . . but *someone* had been there.

What is going on here? I thought.

My answer was only hours away . . . and it would come to me in a terrifying way.

After the men finished unloading the heavy furniture, I spent most of the afternoon carrying smaller boxes from the moving truck into our hew house. After everything was brought inside, I stayed in my new bedroom the rest of the day—on the second floor opposite the playroom—unpacking and getting things organized. It was a big job.

For dinner, Dad called for a pizza to be delivered. We ate in the living room amid a pile of boxes.

"I have a question," I said as I reached for another slice of pizza.

Mom and Dad looked at me. "What's that?" Dad asked.

"When we came and looked at the house that very first time, did you see a white cat in the living room?"

Dad chewed his pizza and thought for a moment. Then, he looked at Mom and shook his head.

"I didn't see a cat," he said.

Mom shook her head, too. "No," she said. "Why? Did you see a cat?"

"I saw a white cat sitting on the couch, right here in the living room," I said. "He was all white with one black ear."

"Maybe it belonged to Mr. Hooper," Mom said.

I shook my head. "I asked him today. He said he had a cat, but it was when he was little."

"It was probably just a pillow," Dad said.

"Or maybe you're going crazy," Clay said.

I ignored him. "No, it was a real, live cat," I said. "I saw him move."

"It must have been something else," Dad said. "I

didn't see any cat toys or litter box."

I dropped the subject. I was sure I'd seen a cat, whether anyone else saw it or not. I know a real, live cat when I see one.

I was tired, so I went to bed just after nine o'clock. It had been a long day, and the next day would be just as busy.

As I crawled into bed, I remembered that strange voice in my head—the voice I'd heard the very first day we'd visited the home.

Don't go inside. Don't go near that house.

"Is something wrong?" Mom asked as she came into my room. "You look worried about something."

I smiled thinly. "No," I said. "I'm fine."

Mom leaned over, kissed my cheek, and pulled the covers up to my chin. "See you in the morning," she said. "We have another big day tomorrow. There's still lots to unpack."

"See ya," I said, and I closed my eyes, unaware that it was the beginning of a long, horrifying night.

I was awakened by a noise.

I opened my eyes and sat up in bed. I was confused for a moment, and a little frightened. It was dark, but the sun had just set and there was still a faint orange glow in the western sky.

What's going on? I thought sleepily.

I was in a bedroom . . . but it wasn't *my* bedroom. In *my* bedroom, the window was on the left side of the bed, not the right.

And there were boxes on the floor. How did they get there?

Then, it suddenly came to me.

We moved. We're in our new home. I'm in my new bedroom.

But, I'd heard a noise, I was sure. That's what woke me.

Still sitting up, I listened intently. The only thing I could hear was the faint sound of the television downstairs. Mom and Dad were still up. I looked at the glowing numbers of my clock radio on the table next to my bed. It was only ten o'clock, so I hadn't been sleeping for long.

Just as I was about to lay back in bed, the noise came again.

Creeeeee. . . .

The sound was long and slow. It was the unmistakable sound of a door opening.

My eyes widened as I peered into the gloom through my open bedroom door. It hadn't been *my* door that had moved. A chill flowed through my body like cold electricity as I listened to the strange sound.

. . . eeeeaaak . . . .

Then, it stopped.

It's my brother, I told myself. *It has to be. His bedroom is on this floor, across the hall just a little ways down from mine.*

I waited, expecting to see a light come on. Maybe he was getting up to get a glass of water.

Creeeeeeeaaaaak . . . .

The sound caused yet another tingling chill to sweep through my body.

"Clay?" I whispered.

I was answered by silence.

"Clay? Is that you?"

There was no answer, and I was getting a little freaked out . . . especially since I was in our new home, and it was the middle of the night.

But I also knew there had to be a logical reason for the noise. Something was causing the creaking sound.

What was it?

Creeeeeeeeaaaaaak . . . .

I pulled the covers down and slowly swung my legs off the bed. My bare feet touched the cool wood floor. I stood and listened.

Silence.

Slowly, I tiptoed across the floor until I reached

the doorway. The hall was completely dark, except for a thin bar of faint light escaping through Clay's partially opened bedroom door. Clay still didn't like to sleep in darkness, so he had a small night light plugged into the wall near his bed.

I listened, but heard nothing except the noise from the television in the downstairs living room. Then:

Creeeeeeeeeeeeeek . . . .

The noise caused me to flinch because it was so close.

I reached out, found my bedroom light switch, flicked it up . . . and placed my hand over my mouth to keep from screaming.

The door of the playroom at the end of the hall was closing by itself! It was closing by itself . . . and I wasn't anywhere near the weak floorboards!

16

I stood in the doorway, bathed in the yellow glow of my bedroom light. The door to the playroom continued to open.

. . . eeeeaaaaak . . . .

My heart throbbed and my stomach was doing back flips.

How could the door to the playroom open all by itself? I wondered. True, if you stood on the floorboards in front of the door, the weak wood caused the door to open and close. But there was nothing there!

Terrified, I stood motionless. My eyes darted into the dark playroom. I wondered if Clay might be hiding behind the door, playing a trick on me. Maybe he was getting ready to jump out and scare me.

"Clay?" I whispered. Which was a silly thing to do. If he was trying to play a trick on me, he wasn't going to answer.

But someone—or something—caused that door to move.

I looked down the hall. It was dimly lit from the light that spilled from my bedroom, and the only things I could see were the two large chandeliers and the door to my brother's bedroom, which was open just a few inches. Clay was in there, I was sure. Downstairs, the television squawked.

So, how did the door open all by itself?

It couldn't . . . and that's all there was to it. Something must have caused the door to move. Maybe a draft. Maybe the house settling. Dad said old homes like this one can settle for years and years and years, making strange squeaks and noises in the night. Some people hear these noises and think their home is haunted. They think the noises are caused by ghosts. Which is impossible, of course. Ghosts aren't real. Everyone knows that.

I stood in the doorway for another minute, waiting to see if the door would move. It didn't.

Oh, well, I thought. *Maybe that's just something I'll have to get used to. Maybe the house is still settling, causing the door to move on its own. It's probably nothing to be afraid of.*

I switched off my light, turned, and began to walk to my bed.

I stopped.

At the bottom of my bed, laying on the bedspread, was a white cat. A white cat—with one black ear.

17

There was no mistaking what I was looking at. It was the same cat I'd seen on our first tour of the house. This time, however, the cat wasn't sleeping. He was curled on the bed, but his head was raised. Although his eyes were concealed in shadows, I could tell he was looking at me.

And his tail was moving, swishing slowly like a reed in the wind.

I blinked and rubbed my eyes, thinking that

when I opened them, the cat would be gone. Nope. When I opened my eyes, the cat was still at the foot of my bed.

"Where did you come from?" I whispered.

The cat continued to swish his tail slowly from side to side.

I took a step toward the bed, thinking the cat might get scared and run off. He didn't. He remained right where he was on the bed, like he belonged there.

Mr. Hooper said he had a white cat with a single black ear, I thought. *But that was years and years ago. This couldn't be the same cat.*

Unless—

No. No way. There are no such things as ghosts . . . and certainly no such things as ghost cats.

I padded slowly to the bed, and the cat stayed where he was, swishing his tail slowly. I reached out and gently patted his head. His fur was soft.

"How did you get here, buddy?" I whispered as I scratched behind his ears. He purred.

"You sure are cute," I said. *"But I don't know if my mom and dad would let me have a cat."*

I wondered what to do. Should I go downstairs and tell Mom and Dad about the cat? If I did, they might put him out, and I didn't want that to happen.

So, I decided I would climb back into bed. If the cat wanted to stay, I would let him. If he left, that would be okay, too. He would turn up in the morning. Maybe I could convince Mom and Dad that we should keep him.

"Would you like to stay with us, Mr. Kitty?" I said. *"Do you want to stay here and be our pet?"*

Then, another thought occurred to me: maybe *he* wasn't the one staying with *us*. Maybe it was the other way around. Maybe this was his home before it became ours. Maybe *we* were staying with *him*.

I pulled the covers back, and the cat showed no signs of moving. In fact, he lowered his head and tail like he was going to go to sleep.

I raised my leg and was about to climb into bed. As I did, I looked out the window and into the yard two stories below. There was still a murky orange glow in the western sky, and I could see part of the garden and a few trees. I could see the old cemetery in the distance.

And that's where I saw something else: the form of a person, standing in the gloom near the cemetery gate!

It was only a dark silhouette, but there was no mistaking it for anything other than a person. He was small, too, and suddenly I remembered the boy I'd spotted earlier in the day. I thought it had been Clay, but it wasn't.

What's he doing in the cemetery? I thought.

The boy moved. He began walking toward our house, but he was still too far away to make out any features.

I became nervous and a little scared. *Who is he?* I wondered. *I should tell Mom and Dad. No one should be in our yard after dark.*

The boy turned and continued walking until I could no longer see him. Then, I walked to the window to see where he was headed.

He was gone.

Oh, he was still in the yard somewhere, I was sure. But I couldn't see him.

That's it, I thought. *I'm telling Mom and Dad. They need to know about the kid in the yard. And I should probably tell them about the cat, too.*

I found my slippers beneath my bed and stepped into them.

"You stay right here," I whispered to the cat as I gave him a pat on his head. *"I'll be right back. And don't worry: I won't let Mom or Dad put you outside."*

I turned and started to walk. The bottoms of my slippers made a soft swishing sound against the wood floor, and I bumped into a box and nearly fell. I knelt down and pushed it aside, so I wouldn't trip over it again. I stood . . . and froze.

The boy that had been in the yard was standing in my doorway!

I nearly screamed . . . but I stopped myself before I did. It was a good thing, too, because the figure in the doorway wasn't the person I'd seen in the yard—it was only my brother, Clay! He was wearing his pajamas that had cartoon monsters all over. His hair was messy, and he looked groggy.

"What are you doing there?!?!" I hissed, and my voice trembled.

"I could ask you the same thing," Clay replied.

"Where are you going?"

"I saw someone in the yard," I whispered. *"I was going to tell Mom and Dad."*

"Why are we whispering?" Clay asked. "Mom and Dad are downstairs. The television is on. They can't hear us."

Good point.

"I saw someone by the cemetery," I said. "He walked through our yard, but I don't know where he went. And look—"

I turned and pointed.

The cat was gone!

"At what?" Clay asked.

"There was a white cat on my bed just a few seconds ago!" I said, still pointing at my bed. "He was right there!"

Clay reached over and flicked on my bedroom light. I knelt down and looked under the bed: no cat. I looked around the room.

Nothing.

He was gone. It was like he was never there.

"There was a white cat on my bed just a few seconds ago," I said. "He looked like the same cat I saw the first time we came to the house."

"You've lost your marbles," Clay said.

"I have not!" I hissed.

Clay strode to my bedroom window. "Where did you see the kid?"

I walked to his side and looked out the window, but it was difficult to see anything outside, due to the glare in the glass caused by my bedroom light. I went over to the door and turned off the light, then returned to the window.

"He was over there," I said, pressing a finger to the glass as I pointed to the old cemetery in the distance. "He was by the fence, and then he started coming toward our house. But I don't know where he went. And now it's getting too dark to see anything."

"You should still tell Mom and Dad, though," Clay said. "But if you tell them there was a cat on your bed, they're going to think you're crazy."

"I'm telling you, he was right there," I said, pointing at the foot of my bed. "He was curled up right there. He's all white, with one black ear, and he's—"

"Yeah, sure," Clay said. "Whatever. I'm going back to bed."

He turned and padded back into his bedroom.

I knelt down, got on my hands and knees, and

looked under the bed.

No cat.

And my closet door was closed, so he couldn't get in there.

I stood and looked behind the door.

Nope.

Where could he have gone? I wondered. *Cats can't vanish into thin air.*

But, then again, maybe this one *could*.

I kicked off my slippers. I was just about to climb back into bed when I turned and looked out the window . . . and what I saw caused my entire body to go numb with terror.

In the yard below, drifting over the lawn like a cloud, was a ghost.

Not a human-shaped ghost, but a weird, flowing white creature with a large, round mouth open in a silent scream. His arms—or what appeared to be arms—were stretched wide, and they hung limp.

And I couldn't be sure . . . but the thing appeared to be staring up at me!

While I watched, the ghostly figure began to

move. It drifted back toward the cemetery, floating, balloon-like. I couldn't turn my eyes from the horrifying sight. The thing appeared to be looking directly at me! By the time it reached the cemetery, it was quickly swallowed by dark shadows.

I tore out of my room and raced down the hall with blinding fury. My bare feet pounded on the wood floor.

"Mom!" I shrieked. *"Dad! There's a ghost in the backyard! There's a ghost in the backyard!"* I raced down the steps, still yelling.

I could hear noises from somewhere in the house, downstairs. Then, I heard a flurry of footsteps.

"He's in the backyard!" I said as I reached the bottom of the stairs. "He's in the backyard!"

Mom and Dad had rushed out of the living room and met ,e at the stairs.

"What on earth are you talking about?" Mom asked. Both she and Dad had worried looks on their faces.

"A ghost!" I said. "I saw him in the backyard!"

"A ghost?" Dad said with a frown. I could tell by the tone of his voice that he didn't believe me.

I hurried to the kitchen window and looked

outside, but it was too dark to see anything. By now, Clay had heard all the commotion and was coming down the steps.

"I watched him go back to where the cemetery is," I continued. "Then, he disappeared."

Mom and Dad looked out the window.

"It wasn't a ghost, Hannah," Mom said.

"It had to be!" I insisted. "It was white, and it floated in the air. It went to the cemetery!"

"There are no such things as ghosts," Dad said. "But I'd better have a look, anyway."

He opened a drawer and pulled out a large, black flashlight. Then, he walked to the back door, opened it, and stopped. He flicked on the back porch light and looked around outside.

"I don't see anything," he said. "But I'll check it out."

Dad turned on the flashlight and stepped outside and into the night.

"I hope the ghost doesn't get him," I said. "That thing looked scary."

"You may have seen something," Mom said, "but I don't think it was a ghost. There must be another explanation."

"He sure looked like a ghost to me," I said. "He was really freaky-looking."

"Well, I'm not sure what you saw," Mom said, "but I'm sure it wasn't a ghost."

Mom, Clay, and I peered out the open back door. We could see Dad making his way through the yard, sweeping the flashlight beam from side to side as he made his way closer and closer to the cemetery. Soon, we couldn't see him at all. The only thing we could see was the flashlight beam.

"He's right at the spot where I saw the ghost disappear," I said.

And that's when the flashlight went out . . . and Dad screamed.

21

"*What happened to Dad!?!?*" Clay shrieked.

"I don't know," Mom said. She sounded worried. "Stay here," she ordered, and she stepped outside and onto the porch.

Dad was no longer screaming, and we couldn't hear anything except a few crickets chirping and the tinny sound of the television in the living room.

"What's happened to Dad?" I asked. I was really worried. We *all* were. I'd never heard Dad scream like that, ever.

"I'll be right back," Mom said. "Stay in the house."

Clay and I stood by the open door, watching Mom as she walked cautiously across the gloomy backyard. The moon had started to rise, and Mom's dark shadow followed her across the grass as she left the glow of the back porch light.

We haven't even been here one night, I thought, *and I'm already totally freaked out by this place.*

I started thinking about the strange things that had happened: seeing the white cat on the very first day and then seeing him on my bed just a short time ago, seeing the boy in the cemetery, and seeing the strange creature or ghost or whatever it was in our backyard. Dad had gone outside to find out what it was . . . and something awful had happened to him.

Suddenly, we saw a flashlight beam appear by the cemetery. The beam's movements were hurried and jerky. Mom stopped in the yard, and soon we could see Dad's shadowy figure appear.

"Are you all right?" Mom called out.

"Yeah," Dad said sheepishly. He met Mom in the yard, and they walked toward us.

"Did the ghost attack you?" I asked.

Dad shook his head. He and Mom stepped onto the back porch and came inside.

"I got surprised by a big raccoon," Dad said with a sheepish grin. "I surprised him, and he surprised me. I don't know who was more scared."

"What about the ghost?" I asked.

Dad shook his head and put the flashlight on the counter. "I didn't see anything," he said. "Are you sure you weren't dreaming?"

"I was wide awake," I said. "You can ask Clay."

"Well, whatever it was, it's gone now. Don't worry. All the doors and windows are locked, so nothing can get in. Not even a raccoon."

But Dad was wrong. Things *could* get through the doors and windows. Locks weren't going to stop the things that were, at that very moment, slipping in and out of our home . . . .

22

I didn't say anything to Mom or Dad about the cat. I figured they'd think I was crazy. After all: the animal had seemingly vanished from my bedroom.

But I hoped I would find him somewhere. He was cute, and I was hoping we could keep him as a pet.

Clay and I went back to bed. Dad said he'd have a look around in the morning, during the daylight. Again, he told us not to worry.

But I did. I worried. I couldn't help it. Before going to bed, I looked out the window, staring, searching the moonlit yard for any sign of the strange thing I'd seen. I saw nothing.

Later, as I lay in bed, I stared at the ceiling for a long time, wondering what was going on. *How did the white cat with the black ear mysteriously appear in my bedroom? How had he disappeared? Who . . . or what . . . had been in our backyard? Why?*

Weird. Just plain *weird.*

The next morning, after breakfast, Dad went outside and hunted around the backyard and the old cemetery.

"I didn't see anything out of the ordinary," he said as he strode into the kitchen. "Maybe it was just a neighbor, walking home."

"At night?" I asked.

Dad shrugged. "I wouldn't worry about it, Hannah," Dad said. "We're safe here."

He was right. Whatever I'd seen in the yard last night, it probably wasn't a ghost. That didn't explain the cat, but I was sure there was some explanation for that, too. After all: if the cat had been living here for a long time, he probably knew all the hiding places. He knew how to get in and around without anyone seeing him. Cats are good like that.

I helped Mom wash the breakfast dishes, and Dad and Clay cleaned the kitchen.

"I'd like you to finish getting your room organized today," Mom said to me as I dried a plate. "Unpack the rest of the clothes from the boxes, and put them away."

"Okay," I said. I was actually looking forward to it. My new bedroom was a lot bigger than the one at our old house. I had a lot more room for hanging pictures and posters.

Dad spoke. "Clay," he said, "go and change into some old clothes. There's a lot of dead branches I want to trim from some of the trees in the yard. I'd like you to haul them back to the woods at the edge of our property."

"Okeydokey," Clay said, and he left the kitchen and went upstairs.

"I'm going to get to work in the garden out back," Mom said. "There are a lot of weeds to pull."

I went up to my room and changed into a pair of jeans and a red T-shirt with white letters that read: *Flying Monkeys Stole My Homework!*

I looked outside. Dad and Clay were in the backyard. Both were wearing leather gloves, and Dad was carrying a handsaw. The sky was overcast and gray.

I pushed up my bedroom window about six inches to let some fresh air in. There was no screen, so I'd have to remember to close it before I went to bed. I didn't want a bunch of mosquitos getting into my room and biting me while I slept.

"I'll be out back in the garden, Hannah," Mom shouted from downstairs.

"Okay," I shouted back. "When I get done putting my clothes away, I'll come out and help."

I heard the back door close. In my window, Mom appeared in the yard below. She walked over to the garden and got to work.

I looked at the boxes stacked near my dresser. There were also a bunch of boxes we'd placed in the playroom. Some of those were mine, and some were Clay's. I figured it wouldn't take too long to put everything away.

And that's when I heard the door creaking again. It was the same sound I'd heard the night before.

Creeeeeeeeaaaaaaaak . . . .

Slowly, I tiptoed to my bedroom door. My heart was pounding, but I really wasn't all that worried. I just figured I'd have to get used to the playroom door opening and closing all by itself.

I stood in my doorway, staring across the hall. The door to the playroom was open only a tiny bit. It was no longer moving.

Then, I saw something move at the bottom of the door, and my skin tingled.

As I watched, the cat walked through the solid wood door and was now sitting in the middle of the hall, staring up at me!

I back-stepped into my bedroom. My mouth hung open in a silent gasp, and my skin broke out in tingling goose bumps.

This isn't real! I thought. *This can't be happening!*

The white cat with the black ear sat in the middle of the hall, slowly swishing his tail back and forth. He looked so sweet and cute and innocent . . . but I was horrified.

Cats can't walk through doors, I thought. *Nothing*

can walk through doors—except . . . .

Ghosts.

I took another step back, and the cat stood. He followed me into my bedroom and sat on the floor.

"What . . . what in the world are you?" I stammered nervously. "Are you a real cat? Where did you come from? How did you walk through the door?"

As if he could understand me, the cat let out a soft meow. His tail continued to swish methodically back and forth.

I took several more steps back and sat on my bed. The cat stood, walked to my feet, and leapt onto my lap. I could feel his paws on my legs as he turned and rubbed his side against my stomach.

Cautiously, I began to stroke his back. He responded by meowing and pressing harder against my stomach.

Gradually, my fear went away. Whatever the cat was, whatever he was doing, he wasn't going to hurt me.

A ghost cat, I thought. Sure, it was crazy, but that's the only explanation I had. *Real* cats would never be able to walk through something solid like a door. And yet, I had watched it happen with my very own eyes.

I looked out the window. Mom was kneeling in the garden, and Dad and Clay were at a nearby tree. Dad was sawing a dead branch, and Clay was waiting for it to fall so he could carry it away.

I thought about picking up the cat and taking him outdoors. Would they be able to see him, like I could? After all: they didn't see the cat sitting on the couch when we first toured the house.

Maybe I'm the only one who can see him, I thought. *That would be super-weird.*

At that moment, I heard the playroom door creaking again. I was about to get up and take a look, but I never got the chance.

Suddenly, the ghostly figure of a boy was standing in my bedroom doorway! When he saw me, his jaw fell. He pointed at me . . . and started screaming!

24

I was so shocked by what I was seeing and hearing that I jumped and almost knocked the cat from my lap. The boy just stood there, staring at me, pointing and screaming. But his voice was very distant, like he was far away. It was really odd. Although he was standing in my doorway only a few feet from me, his shrieking sounded like he could have been on the next block.

And I noticed that his form was different, too. He didn't appear to be a solid figure. The more I stared, the more I realized I could see right through him! I could actually see right through his body!

Suddenly, he stopped screaming, turned, and ran down the hall. I noticed something else that was strange: his footsteps made no sound at all. In seconds, the boy was gone. It was like he had never been there.

The cat was still on my lap, and he leapt to the floor. He sauntered to the doorway, sat, and looked at me.

This is totally crazy, I thought. *Is it me? Am I losing my mind?*

No, I wasn't. I knew what I saw. I knew what I heard.

And I was going to do whatever it took to convince Mom and Dad. I knew they might think I'd gone crazy, but I was going do whatever it took to make them believe me. Something—I didn't know what—was very wrong with this house. Too many weird things were going on. In fact, we might all be in danger and not even know it.

The cat was still sitting in my doorway, and I walked over to him. He didn't try to get away as I picked him up; rather, I think he liked it. He purred a couple of times as I cradled him in my arms.

My plan was to take him outside to Mom and Dad. They would *have* to see him, I was sure. That wouldn't explain the other things that were happening, but if I could show them the cat and tell them about the strange boy, maybe they would believe me.

I never got that far.

As I walked down the steps carrying the cat, a very strange feeling came over me. Like someone was watching me.

Like someone was *waiting*.

I slowed as I reached the last few steps, and when I looked into the kitchen, my blood ran cold. My skin felt like ice.

Six people were sitting around the kitchen table . . . *six people I had never seen before in my life!*

25

I stopped walking and stared at the six people seated around the table. There were two men, the boy I'd seen upstairs, two women, and a young girl, probably a couple of years younger than me. The women and the girl were wearing old-fashioned dresses, and the men were wearing black pants with white shirts. The expressions on their faces were shock and horror. They all appeared to be staring in my direction, but they weren't looking at me . . . they were looking at the cat.

It was as if they could see the cat, but not me!

The boy spoke, but his voice was so faint that I couldn't hear what he said. He pointed in my direction and continued talking.

I got up enough nerve, and spoke. "What are you doing in our house?" I asked.

One of the women flinched and said something, but, like the boy's screams had been, her voice seemed distant and far away. Their eyes never left the cat I cradled in my arms.

That must look crazy, I thought. *If they can see the cat, but can't see me, it must look like the animal is floating in the air!*

And I realized all of the people around the table were like the boy, in the fact that I could actually see right through them.

I'm dreaming, I thought. *That's the only explanation there can be. I'm having a dream, and I'll wake up soon.*

So, I figured if I was having a dream, I had absolutely nothing to worry about. I took a breath . . . and walked up to the table.

The people continued staring at the cat in my arms, and I was sure they couldn't see me. I bent down and put the cat on the floor. Their eyes followed the cat as it walked to the bottom of the staircase and sat.

I waved my arms around, trying to get their attention. They didn't see me.

"Can you guys see me at all?" I asked.

That seemed to get their attention, as all of the people around the table flinched. The young girl spoke.

"I heard something!" she said. She looked more horrified than ever.

They all looked around me, but not *at* me.

"I'm right here," I said. "Right in front of you." I waved my hands in front of one of the men, but he couldn't see it.

Finally, I spoke in a raised voice. *"I'm right HERE!"* I shouted.

When I said the word 'here,' all six people freaked out! Their eyes just about popped out of their heads! One of the men gasped. A lady on the other side of the table quickly covered her mouth with her hands to stifle a scream.

"Sorry," I said. "I didn't mean to scare you."

"Go away!" one of the men shouted. His eyes darted all over the room, but never directly at me. "Leave our home and never come back!"

Our home? I thought. *It's not their home . . . it's ours. What was he talking about?*

Clearly, they were terrified. I couldn't figure out why they would be so afraid of me. Still, none of them were looking directly at me, and I again realized they couldn't see me.

Then again, I couldn't figure out how six strange people were in our house . . . until it finally sunk in.

I'm not dreaming, I thought. *They're ghosts, Hannah. That's what they are. And, for some reason, they must think I'm a ghost, too!*

I'd had enough. I knew I wasn't dreaming, and I was totally freaked out. I wanted out of the house, and fast.

I turned, ran to the back door, grabbed the knob and tried to turn it . . . but it wouldn't budge. I checked the lock, but it wasn't engaged.

I turned and looked into the kitchen.

The ghost-people had risen from their seats. They were all looking at me . . . or through me, I couldn't tell.

"Go away, whoever you are!" one of the men shouted. *"Go away and never come back!"*

And that's what I wanted to do. I wanted out of the house as fast as possible. I wanted to run and run and run.

But I couldn't.

The house wouldn't let me. It was keeping me inside . . . and as I tried the door again, I realized there was no way out.

26

Suddenly, the door burst open. It happened so quickly that I turned and almost fell.

Dad!

He was standing on the back porch, holding the door open, looking at me with wide eyes and a look of confusion. He had been trying to come inside, while I had been trying to get out. That's why I thought I had been trapped. I couldn't get the door open because he had been holding the knob on the opposite side.

"What's wrong?" he asked. "I heard you shouting something."

"Them!" I shouted. "That's what's wrong!" I pointed behind me and turned my head.

The people were gone! They had vanished!

"They were right there, honest!" I shrieked frantically. My eyes darted around the room. "There were six people, sitting at the table! They were coming after me!"

Dad stepped through the door and looked around. "What are you talking about?" he asked. "There's no one here, Hannah."

"There were six people sitting at the table!" I insisted. My heart was thumping, and I was gulping deep breaths. "There . . . there was a boy and a girl and four grown-ups!"

Dad looked at me like I was a space alien. "Hannah, you've got to stop making things up," he said.

"I'm not making anything up!" I insisted. "A boy came through the door of the playroom upstairs. When I came down here, he was sitting at the table with five other people! I think they were ghosts!"

Again, Dad looked around. Then, he smiled and

put his hand on my shoulder. "You and your imagination," he said.

It was no use. Dad wasn't going to believe me, no matter what I said. Unless—

I turned my head and saw the cat sitting at the foot of the stairs.

"Look!" I said, pointing. "There's the cat, right there!"

Dad looked where I was pointing.

"What are you talking about?" Dad asked. "What cat?"

"Right there, by the stairs!" I replied. "Can't you see him?!?!"

Dad rolled his eyes. "Really, Hannah," he said, "you've *got* to stop making things up. Aren't you supposed to be organizing your bedroom?"

"You . . . you really can't see the cat?" I said, bewildered.

"There's no cat there," Dad said. Then, he looked at me, and a look of concern fell over his face. He put his hands on my shoulders. "Are you feeling all right?" he asked.

"I'm fine," I said. "It's just that—"

I stopped in mid-sentence. I knew that unless

Dad had proof, unless he actually *saw* some of these things himself, he wasn't going to believe me.

"What?" Dad asked.

"Never mind," I said with a frustrated shrug. "I'm fine. I really am."

"Okay," Dad said. "When you get done with your room, your mother could use some help in the garden. There's a lot that needs to be done."

"All right," I said with a nod.

Dad walked past me, pulled a glass from the cupboard, and filled it with water from the faucet. I looked at him, then at the cat.

Dad can't see the cat, I thought. *That's totally creepy.*

He finished his water and placed the empty glass in the sink. Just then, the cat meowed.

Dad stopped and turned his head.

"What was that?" he asked curiously.

"You heard it?" I said.

"I heard something," he replied.

"That was the cat!" I said hopefully. "He's right there! I'll show you!"

I ran to the foot of the stairs to pick up the cat. Maybe Dad couldn't see him, but he might be able to feel him.

But the cat got spooked. He bounded up the steps and vanished.

"You and your imagination," Dad said again, shaking his head. "Finish your room, and I'll see you in the backyard." He pushed the back door open, stepped outside, and closed the door behind him.

I stood at the foot of the stairs, looking around. I was confused and scared. I knew I hadn't imagined seeing the boy or those people. I knew I'd seen the cat. In fact, I'd even *felt* the animal in my lap and in my arms.

Finally, after a few minutes, I got the nerve to go back up the stairs. As I walked, I looked warily around, afraid I might see someone—or something—at any moment. Thankfully, I didn't.

But I hadn't reached my bedroom yet . . . and that's where, once again, something was waiting for me.

27

Have you ever had a feeling that something was about to go horribly wrong? Like something bad was about to happen, but you didn't know what it was?

That's how I felt as I walked down the hall toward my bedroom. I could sense something wasn't right. Of course, I *knew* that already, because I'd seen the strange boy and the people downstairs. And the cat. Apparently, I was the only person who could see them.

Now, as I walked down the hall, I slowed. I walked carefully, quietly, so I could listen for any strange sounds. The only thing I could hear was the faint sound of Dad sawing a tree branch in the yard.

When I reached the playroom, I peered around the open door. There was nothing to see but boxes that still needed to be unpacked. However, I stepped on the weak floorboards and the door started to close. The squeaking sound made me nearly jump out of my skin!

I breathed a sigh of relief, turned, and looked into my room. There was no sign of the cat, nor did anything appear to be unusual. Outside, I heard a branch fall to the ground, and Dad calling out to Clay.

Still, that uneasy feeling gnawed at me. There was something wrong with this house, I was sure. After all: I had been warned. On the very first day, there had been a voice in my head.

Don't go inside. Don't go near that house.

I had thought it was only my imagination, but now I knew there was much more to it than that.

Don't go inside. Don't go near that house.

Still wary, I took a step into my room . . . and that's when I heard it.

A scratching sound.

I stopped and looked around. Nothing moved. Below, in the yard outside, I saw Clay hauling away a large tree branch. Dad had started sawing again, but I couldn't see him from where I stood.

Again, I heard the sound of scratching. It was very faint, and it sounded like it was coming from the other side of my room. However, I couldn't see it because my bedroom door was halfway closed.

Fear trickled down my spine.

Should I get Mom and Dad? I wondered. *No,* I thought. *They'll never believe me. After all: Dad didn't believe that I'd seen six people in our house. He hadn't seen the cat, even though I'd been able to see it as plain as day. He'd get mad if I told him I was hearing things in my bedroom.*

So, I decided to find out what was making the noise. I told myself it was probably just the cat.

Slowly, I reached out and pushed my bedroom door. It creaked as it opened.

Again, I heard the scratch, followed by a fluttering sound. I kept pushing the door open . . . and suddenly, a small dark form attacked, coming right at my face!

The thing came at me so fast that I didn't have a chance to move . . . and it hit me in the forehead! I shrieked and leapt away, swatting my hands in the air in front of my face. I heard a fluttering of wings and frantic chirping.

It was a bird!

A small brown bird had flown into my room—through my open bedroom window—and couldn't find his way out! He was probably more afraid of me than I was of him!

After I caught my breath, I closed my bedroom door so he wouldn't fly through the house. I hurried across the room and pushed the window up all the way, to give the bird a bigger space to escape.

The bird was sitting on one of the boxes piled near my bed. His whole body was trembling, and I felt sorry for him. The poor thing was terrified.

"Don't worry," I said, "I know what it's like to be scared." I swept my arm toward the window. "Go on," I said. "Fly away."

The bird remained seated on the box, still quaking with fear.

I took a step toward him, and that was all it took. The bird darted into the air, chirping like mad. He zipped out the window in a flash and vanished.

I sat on my bed. "I've had just about enough excitement for one day," I said out loud. I was still shaking, and it took me a few minutes to calm down.

Finally, I continued unpacking boxes and putting things away. Mostly, it was just clothing that needed to be put in my dresser or hung up in my closet. There was also a box of games and a few dolls that I've had for a long time. I don't play with the dolls anymore, but I've had them since I was little. I didn't want to throw them away or take them to the thrift store, which is what we do when we outgrow our clothes.

I put the dolls in my closet, but there wasn't any room for my games. So, I figured I would put them underneath my bed, until I found a better place for them.

I knelt down, carrying several board games in my arms. I pulled the blanket up . . . and cried out.

The ghost boy was under my bed!

29

The board games fell from my arms. One of them broke open, and fake paper money and plastic coins went all over the place.

The boy beneath my bed was staring at me with wide eyes. Clearly, he was just as afraid of me as I was of him. But again, he didn't look solid, and the more I looked, the more I realized I could see right through him.

"Don't hurt me," he said. "Please don't hurt me."

"I'm not going to hurt you," I said. My voice was trembling. "What are you doing in my room?"

"That's what I was going to ask you," he said. "Are . . . are you a ghost?"

"Me? A ghost?" I replied. "Of course not. *You're* the ghost."

"I'm not a ghost," the boy said. "I live here. This is my house."

"This is *my* house," I replied. "We just moved here."

"This is very strange," he said. "But it's happened before. A lot."

"What?" I asked. "What's happened before?"

"We see strange people around our home," he replied. "People we don't know. We don't see them all the time. I've seen you a couple of times, but then you just fade away like smoke."

"I've seen you do the same thing!" I said. "That's why I think you're a ghost!"

"That's why I think *you're* a ghost!" he said.

Suddenly, I heard Clay's voice from down the hall.

"Hannah? Mom wants to know why you screamed." He appeared in my doorway. "And who are you talking to?"

I was still kneeling on the floor, holding the bed spread up. "Clay . . . can you see him?"

Clay leaned down and looked under my bed. The boy was still there.

"See who?" Clay said.

"The boy under the bed," I replied, pointing with my free hand.

Clay frowned. "I knew you were weird," he said, "but I didn't think you were *that* weird."

"You really can't see him?" I asked.

"You've lost your marbles," Clay said. "You've gone completely bonkers."

It was no use arguing. For whatever reason, Clay couldn't see the boy under the bed.

"Well, don't scream any more," Clay said. "Mom and Dad are going to get mad if you scream for no reason." Clay turned, and I heard his footsteps go down the hall and down the stairs.

"Who were you talking to?" the boy beneath the bed asked.

"That was my brother," I said.

"There wasn't anyone there," the boy said.

I looked at him curiously. "You . . . you couldn't

see him?" I asked. "He was standing in the bedroom doorway. You *must* have seen him."

"No," the boy said. "I saw you turn your head and talk to someone. But I didn't see or hear anyone."

Now I was *really* confused. There was no rhyme or reason for what was going on. How come *I* could see the boy, but my brother couldn't? How come I could see the cat, but no one else could?

It was a mystery, all right—a mystery that would take a horrifying turn later that night.

30

I talked with him for a few minutes, and he told me he'd hidden under the bed because he was afraid. I told him there was no reason to be afraid of me, but as he started to get out from under the bed, he began to vanish into thin air. In seconds, it was as if he was never there.

And I began to wonder if Clay was right: maybe I *had* lost my marbles. Maybe I *had* gone completely bonkers, just like he'd said. It was simply crazy that no one else could see or hear the boy or the cat or the other people I'd seen in the kitchen.

So, after the boy was gone, after I picked up the pieces of the board game that had broken open, and after I put away the things in my room, I went outside and helped Mom in the garden. I never told her about the boy or the cat. During dinner, Dad never said anything about the six people I told him I'd seen earlier. And Clay never said anything about me talking to the boy I saw under the bed.

Later that evening, we ate popcorn and watched a movie in the living room. There weren't any pictures on the walls, and the room looked bare. Mr. Hooper had taken his pictures down when he moved, and Mom and Dad hadn't had a chance to put any of ours up yet.

And when I went to bed that night, the mysterious white cat was waiting for me. He was sleeping at the foot of my bed.

"There you are," I whispered. I didn't want anyone to hear me talking. They'd think I was talking to myself again. When the cat heard me, he woke up. His tail wagged slowly back and forth, like a sleepy cobra.

I climbed into bed with the cat at my feet. When

Mom came in to kiss me good night, she never saw him.

"We have another busy day tomorrow," Mom said. "Get lots of sleep."

"I will," I said. Mom gave me a kiss, turned off my bedroom light, and left. Down the hall, I could hear my brother in the bathroom, complaining about how his tube of toothpaste had broken open and he got toothpaste all over his hands and arms.

And the white cat stayed on my bed—that is, until the strange figure appeared once again in the backyard . . . .

I don't know how long I'd been sleeping, but I woke when the cat stirred and began meowing. I sat up in bed, propped up on my elbows. I looked at my clock; it was almost eleven.

Unlike the previous night, there was no moon. My bedroom was very dark, and I could only see vague shadows. I could see the silhouette of the cat at the foot of my bed. He was standing, and I could see his tail wisping back and forth.

"What's wrong?" I whispered as I climbed out of bed.

The cat leapt from the bed and landed on the window sill, where he paced back and forth. I walked to the window and peered out into the inky darkness.

The front of our house was lit by streetlights, but here, in the backyard, there were no lights at all. It was completely dark. I looked up, thinking I might see stars, but there were none. Clouds had moved in, hiding the night sky.

Below me, on the window sill, the cat continued to silently pace back and forth, meowing softly every few seconds.

"What is it?" I asked, trying to see into the backyard. The only things I could see were shadows and the dark shapes of trees and branches.

But after standing at my window and staring for nearly a full minute, I finally *did* see something.

A light.

In the distance—probably in or around the cemetery—a light suddenly blinked on. It wasn't very big, and it looked like only a bright pinprick in the distance. But it was a light, that was for sure.

I was also sure of something else: I was going to

find out what it was. I was going to go to the old cemetery and find out where the light was coming from. Oh, I was scared, all right. More than that, actually. I was *terrified*. But I had to know what was going on. I had to find out, and get proof. Then—and only then—would my parents believe me.

I also knew I could get into trouble. Mom and Dad certainly wouldn't want me going outside after dark, and I'd be in hot water if they found out.

But I *had* to know. I had to find out what was going on. Oh, I tried to tell myself it was nothing. I told myself that, in five minutes, I'd be back in bed.

I should have known better. So far, everything that had happened hadn't really been too scary. I mean . . . seeing the boy and the other people: that was kind of scary, but not super scary.

Now, things were about to change. Things were going to get a lot worse . . . fast.

32

I tiptoed out of my bedroom and into the hall, careful not to step on the floorboards that would cause the door to the playroom to creak open. The white cat followed me, brushing against my ankles.

I continued quietly down the hall and down the stairs. At the last step, I stopped and listened.

Nothing.

I continued across the dark living room, through the kitchen, and to the back door. I had to be careful walking, because the only light came from the glow of a tiny night light plugged into the wall by the television.

When I reached the back door, I quietly unlocked it and pulled it open. The white cat sat on the floor and looked up at me. He made no motion to go out.

I stepped outside into the cool night air and quietly pulled the door closed behind me. In the distance, I could still see the small light in the cemetery.

I started walking. The grass was dew-covered and cold against my feet and ankles.

Ahead of me, in the cemetery, I could still see the faint light, glowing like a large firefly. My mind spun. *Who—or what—was there? Who was in the cemetery in the middle of the night?*

I kept walking slowly. Finally, I reached the cemetery.

In the grass, by one of the gravestones, an lantern glowed. It gave off a yellowish-white light, and the effect it had on the other gravestones was eerie. Strange shadows splayed out onto the damp, shiny grass, and I could even read some of the lettering on a few of the grave markers.

But there was no one around.

Strange, I thought. *There's no one here.*

Of course, lots of strange things had been happening. This was just one more thing to add to the list.

And, just because I couldn't see anyone, it didn't mean I was alone. I'd found that out already in our new house.

"Is anyone here?" I called out. The only thing I heard was the continuous chiming of crickets.

"Hello?" I said. No one answered.

Weird, I thought.

I turned around and began walking back toward my house, when a movement to the right of me caught my eye.

I stopped and squinted, trying to see whatever it was. It was so dark that it was hard to make anything out.

Then, I saw it. A white figure, drifting above the ground, moving across the lawn. And, although it was very dark, I knew one thing for certain: whatever the thing was, it definitely was *not* human!

I covered my mouth with my hands before I had a chance to scream. Oh, I *wanted* to scream, all right. I wanted to scream so loud that it would wake the whole neighborhood. But I didn't.

While I watched, the thing in the yard moved faster and faster. Thankfully, it wasn't coming directly at me . . . but it passed by only a few feet away. The thing was all white with several long, white arms flowing behind it. I could even see his face! He had dark, hollow eyes, and a wide, open mouth, like he was screaming—only no sound came out. In fact, the thing made absolutely no sound at all.

In seconds, it had vanished into the dark shadows, leaving me trembling in horror in the yard.

I hurried through the grass to the back door of the house. Quietly, I slipped inside. The white cat was still sitting on the floor, and he followed me as I made my way through the dark house and back up to my bed.

This place is haunted, I thought as I lay in bed with the covers pulled up to my chin. The white cat leapt onto the window sill, gazing into the dark yard below.

Haunted, I kept thinking. All along, I believed there were no such things as ghosts. Even Mom said so. I tried to believe there was a logical explanation for all of the strange things that had happened.

Now I knew better. I had proof. But how could I show this proof to Mom and Dad if they couldn't see it? They needed to know what was going on. After all, if our house was haunted, we might be in danger. Maybe the ghosts would get mad at us. What were they capable of doing?

Oh, I'd get my answer soon enough. The night wasn't yet over.

Not by a long shot.

I fell asleep, but was awakened again sometime later. This time, however, I awoke on my own . . . or I *thought* I awoke on my own. There hadn't been any noise or anything to disrupt my sleep.

The white cat was still sitting on the window sill. When I rose up on my elbows, he leapt to the floor and scampered to my bedroom doorway, where he sat. It was dark, and he was hard to see, but he appeared to be looking right at me.

Then, the cat turned and darted into the hall. I couldn't be sure, but it looked like he had slipped into the playroom.

I was about to lay back down and try to sleep when the cat suddenly returned. He leapt onto the bed, jumped onto my stomach, and sat. I reached up to pet him, but he leapt away, landing on the floor and darting into the hall.

Does he want me to follow him? I wondered.

I pulled back the covers and swung my feet to the floor, stood, and walked silently into the hall. In the gloom of night, I could see the playroom door was open. I saw the silhouettes and shadows of dark boxes that still needed to be unpacked.

And the cat. He was sitting on the floor, staring at something.

I stepped toward the door, and it began creaking. Quickly, I stepped off the weak floorboards, went into the playroom, and flicked on the light. My eyes burned from the brightness, and I squinted.

There were boxes piled everywhere. Most of them had handwriting on them, like *'tools,'* and *'cleaning supplies,'* and *'books.'*

But the cat wasn't sitting in front of those boxes.

He was sitting in front of the large toy chest that was against the wall. He looked at me, then at the toy chest. Then at me again.

"What?" I asked quietly. "What are you trying to tell me?"

The cat replied by jumping onto the toy chest and sniffing it. Then, he jumped down to the floor and sat facing the trunk with his back to me.

I tiptoed over to him and knelt down.

"Do you want me to open it?" I said as I scratched the back of his neck.

The cat offered a single meow.

Again, that now-familiar tingle of fear crept up my spine. Something told me to be careful. In fact, I began to think I should just leave the toy chest alone and go back to bed. I could come back in the morning and open it.

The cat meowed again, looked at me, then the toy chest.

What could possibly be in there? I wondered. When we first toured the house and Clay had hidden in the chest, it was empty. *Was there something in there now?*

My hand trembled as I reached out and fumbled

with the latch.

The cat swished his tail slowly and meowed.

"Here goes nothing," I said softly. I flipped the latch . . . and lifted the lid.

At first, I wasn't sure what I was seeing. But as I opened the lid farther, I could see that the chest contained old, framed pictures.

I opened the lid until it rested on the wall. Then, I picked up one of the pictures. It was an old black and white photograph. There were several people seated on a porch, and I recognized it as the front porch of our new house. The men were all dressed in dark slacks and light shirts, and the women all wore light dresses. The picture appeared to be very old, because people no longer dressed like that today.

I placed the picture on the floor and picked up another one. It, too, was very old. I counted four people standing in a yard—our front yard. There was a date inscribed at the bottom right corner: *July 13, 1897*.

"Wow," I breathed. *"These pictures are over one hundred years old!"*

I placed the picture on the floor. The white cat peered curiously at it, meowed, and gave his tail a slow, methodical sweep.

I picked up another picture and looked at it. *These are the pictures Mr. Hooper had hanging in the living room,* I thought. *He must have forgotten them.*

I picked up another picture. This one had several people standing in front of a huge old steam locomotive. Thick, black smoke boiled from the main stack. And strangely enough, the picture somehow looked . . . familiar. Had I seen it before? It was certainly possible, since we'd been in Mr. Hooper's house while the pictures were still on his living room wall. But I didn't remember seeing this particular picture.

Odd.

I continued staring at it, until I suddenly realized why it was familiar.

"Oh my gosh!" I hissed. *"Oh my gosh!"*

It wasn't the picture that was familiar to me—it was the people! The people in the picture were the same people I'd seen downstairs in our kitchen! The ones who had told me to leave!

I drew the picture closer and studied the people carefully. There was no doubt about it. Some of the people standing in front of the enormous locomotive were the very same people I'd seen around our dining room table.

And that would mean . . . .

"They really *are* ghosts," I said out loud. "They're the ghosts of the people in the pictures."

I placed the picture on the floor next to the other two, and pulled another one from the chest. It was a picture of a man and a woman in a horse-drawn carriage. They didn't look familiar. I put it on the floor and pulled yet another one out of the toy chest.

This particular picture was a bit odd. It was a picture of our house from long ago. At the bottom right corner, someone had scribbled: *Ester and Rufus—Summer, 1900*. There was no exact date.

But that's not what was odd. What I found strange was that there was no one in the picture except a dark-colored dog chasing a ball. There were no people in the picture.

Why had someone written that it was a picture of Ester and Rufus? Rufus was probably the dog, but where was Ester?

Very strange.

The cat was still sitting on the floor, and I reached down and scratched behind his ears.

"I sure wish you could talk," I said, keeping my voice down so my brother wouldn't hear me speaking.

He already thought I was crazy. If he discovered me talking out loud in the middle of the night, he'd think I'd totally lost my mind and go running to Mom and Dad.

However, it wasn't Clay I needed to be worried about. Because when I looked up, I saw my reflection in the window—but that wasn't all.

In the window, I could clearly see the reflection of a ghostly white figure—a figure standing right behind me!

I was so startled that I nearly dropped the picture I was holding. At first, I thought the figure behind me was Clay . . . but it wasn't. It wasn't the boy I'd seen earlier, either.

It was a *girl*.

She looked to be a little older than me. I couldn't tell her hair color or the color of her clothing because she seemed to glow white.

I spun on the floor and looked up at her. I'm

sure my face was as white as hers!

I glared at her, but she wasn't looking at me. She was looking at the picture in my hand.

"Who . . . who are you?" I stammered.

The ghost girl didn't reply.

I crawled farther away. The cat seemed totally unconcerned. He just sat there and looked at me, then the girl, then me again.

"Are you a . . . a *ghost?*" I managed to ask. Again, the girl didn't reply. If she heard me, she gave no indication. She just continued to stare at the picture I had in my hand.

"Is this yours?" I asked, gesturing with the picture.

Still no response.

Finally, she took her eyes off the picture and looked at me. It was odd: she was looking *at* me, but not really. It was more like she was looking *through* me, like she was looking at the floor or the wall on the other side. Her eyes were vacant and empty. Sad, maybe.

I held out the picture, offering it to her to take. When she didn't, I placed it on the floor next to the cat.

I was starting to get really freaked out. Oh, I

was already quite frightened. But so far, nothing bad had happened. Still, it's not every day you see a ghost—or several of them—in your home.

What if she's mad at me? I thought. *What if I'm not supposed to be going through these pictures?*

The girl suddenly looked up, and a strange thing began to happen. She began to turn into smoke. At least, that's what it looked like. Parts of her body began to drift and float, like she was some sort of fog being. The smoke began to whirl—slowly at first, then picking up speed. Soon, I could no longer see any of her features. The girl was gone, wisping into the air like a twisting cloud. The spinning gray-white mist took the shape of a thin tornado, spinning furiously and silently, not creating a sound. The girl—or whatever she had become—kept getting thinner and thinner. Soon, it looked like there was a long, whirling, white pencil in the room. The top of the pencil began to weave back and forth like a snake, taking on a life of its own.

And if that wasn't freaky enough, what happened next was the most bizarre thing I had ever seen in my entire twelve years on this earth . . . .

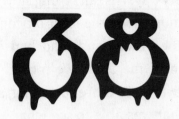

The girl had transformed into a thin, flexible tornado about as big around as my wrist. The top of it began swaying around like a serpent. Then, it began to zip around the room, bouncing off the walls like a snake gone mad! Several times it nearly hit me, and I had to duck. When it finally came so close that it nearly hit my face, I rolled to the side and backed up to get away.

I needn't have worried. The tip of the smoky

snake lowered and touched the picture that I'd just placed on the floor. Somehow, it was being sucked into the glass! The tornado became shorter and shorter, until it finally had vanished altogether.

Meanwhile, the white cat just sat on the floor, looking like everything was cool, like things like this happened every day. His tail swung slowly from side to side, and he didn't look the least bit concerned.

I, on the other hand, had had enough weird things happen to me since we moved into our new home. And it was even more confusing, since I was the only person that was able to see what was going on!

I was still kneeling on the floor. After a moment, I stood and walked to the toy chest. I picked up the picture—the one with Rufus, the dog—and got a surprise I would have never imagined.

39

There was now a girl in the picture!

The same girl that had appeared in the playroom was now in the picture, frozen in time. She was smiling at the dog, and her arm was raised, like she'd just thrown the ball he was chasing.

But, believe it or not, I wasn't all that shocked. Like I've already said: lots of weird things had happened since we'd moved into the new home. I was getting used to strange things happening.

I put the picture aside and continued going through the remaining photographs in the toy chest. There were only six more, and I didn't see anyone else I recognized. I looked for Mr. Hooper the pictures, but I didn't see him anywhere.

I picked up the picture of Ester and Rufus. The girl and the dog looked so happy. And to think: I was looking at a photograph taken over a century ago! Not only that, but I had seen her ghost in this very room!

So strange, I thought. *Every day, things just get weirder and weirder.*

Finally, I returned all the pictures to the toy chest and went back to bed. And while I laid there with my eyes closed, I wondered: *How am I going to get someone to believe me? Who would believe the things that had happened to me over the past couple of days?*

No one, that's who. Unless I had proof, no one was going to believe a word I said about ghosts.

So, I decided the best thing I could do was get a good nights' sleep and collect my thoughts in the morning.

Yep. That would be best. I'll get up in the morning, and I'll make a list of everything that's happened.

While I doubted it would give me answers, at least I would have a written record of what had happened since we moved into our new home. Maybe, if I couldn't make it all make sense to anyone else, I could make it make sense to *me*.

And the fact is, it *would* make sense . . . sort of. The pieces of the puzzle were all going to fall into place—and the truth would be even stranger than I could have ever imagined.

In the morning, I didn't tell Mom or Dad about the things that had happened overnight, as I was sure they wouldn't believe me. Instead, I went up to my room after breakfast and found my notepad. I sat on my bed, writing down everything I'd experienced in our new home: the voice in my head that had told me not to go near the house, the cat no one else could see, the ghost-boy and the other ghost people, the light in the cemetery, and the scary white ghost I'd seen in the backyard. I wrote about the experience I had in the playroom late last night. I tried to remember anything and everything unusual about the house.

And as I read over what I'd written, I still couldn't get anything to make sense. I was no closer to figuring out what was going on.

I heard footsteps on the stairs and in the hall, and Clay appeared at my bedroom door. He was holding his catcher's mitt and a softball.

"Wanna play catch in the yard?" he asked.

"Not right now," I said.

"What are you doing?" he asked.

I told him the truth. "I'm making a list of all the weird things about this house," I replied, very matter-of-factly.

Clay rolled his eyes. "You're still freaked out about this place, huh?" he said.

"Something is going on in this house," I insisted, "and I'm going to find out what it is."

"Fine with me," Clay said with a shrug. "Feel free to waste your time. When you get bored, I'll be in the backyard." He turned, and I heard his footsteps go down the hall and down the stairs.

I re-read what I'd written, trying to piece

together the facts, trying to make sense of the things I'd seen and experienced. It was no use. I was just as confused as ever.

Looking through my bedroom window, I saw Clay below me in the backyard. He tossed his softball high into the air and caught it when it came back down. Then, he threw it again.

Might as well go outside and play catch with Clay, I thought. I put the notepad on my pillow and retrieved my baseball glove from my closet.

Downstairs, Mom and Dad were talking in the kitchen.

"We're going to go down to Home Giant to pick up some things for the house," Dad said. "Clay wants to stay here. Will you stay and look after him? We'll only be gone about fifteen minutes."

I shrugged. "Sure," I said, although I was a bit nervous being alone in the house. But, then again, Clay would be here. Everything would be fine.

I stood on the front porch and waved to Mom and Dad as they drove away. And just as I was about to leap off the porch and go around to the backyard and find Clay, a vehicle pulled into the driveway.

A blue truck.

It stopped by the garage. In the driver's seat, I saw someone wave, but I couldn't tell who it was because of the glare of the glass.

A man got out.

Mr. Hooper.

In a split-second, I decided I would tell him everything that had happened. After all: he'd lived in the home for years and years. Maybe he would have some answers.

Well, he had answers, all right. I was about to find out the truth about our haunted home on Cedar Mill Street.

41

Before Mr. Hooper even had a chance to say 'hello,' I began blurting everything out to him. He stood in the driveway, eyes wide, while I told him about the strange ghost-boy I had actually spoken to. I told him about the other people and the cat and the weird ghost creature in the yard. And I told him what had happened the night before, in the playroom, when I'd found the pictures and the girl turned into a smoky tornado.

Finally, when I was finished, he smiled.

"Most people can't see them," he said. "My sister could, when we were growing up here long ago. But I never could."

I was perplexed. "What do you mean?" I asked. "I thought you said there weren't any ghosts here."

"What you saw aren't really ghosts," he replied, which confused me even more.

"What do you mean?" I replied.

Mr. Hooper frowned. His gray hair shined in the sun, making it appear silver. "Let me explain it this way," he said. "What you saw aren't actually 'ghosts.' They are more like old memories that are still lingering on. They are the memories from years past. They are memories of the old house."

"But what about the pictures?" I asked. "How does a girl turn into smoke and go into an old picture."

"It's like this," Mr. Hooper said. "Pictures stir memories. When you see something you remember, it touches you in a certain way. Understand?"

I did. When I look at pictures of when I was little, I remember what I was doing when the picture was taken. I remember the fun I had, and it makes me feel good.

"That's what this house does with those pictures. It's the *house* that remembers all those good memories. In fact, that's the reason I came by today. When I was packing my things, I put all of my pictures in the toy chest so they wouldn't get broken. I was going to pack them in a special, padded box . . . but I forgot. I was hoping I could pick them up today."

"If you take them away, will I see any more ghosts?" I asked.

Mr. Hooper shook his head. "Not ghosts," he said. "Memories. And no, when the pictures are gone, the memories will be gone. They'll no longer be the memories of this house. They'll be my memories. I just don't have the ability to see them the way you and my sister do. In fact, very few people can see them."

As crazy as it sounded, what Mr. Hooper told me seemed to make sense.

"How is it that I can see these things, but Mom and Dad and my brother can't?" I asked.

"There are some people who have the ability to see these memories," Mr. Hooper explained. "You aren't alone. My sister could see them, but most people can't. You should consider yourself very special."

"But what about the cat?" I said with a bit of

sadness. After all: I'd gotten a little attached to him. If he was gone, I would miss him.

"Snowflake's memory has lingered in this house for years and years," Mr. Hopper said. "I think, with your ability, you'll see him around a lot."

"So, it really *is* your cat?" I asked.

"Yes," the old man replied. "You described Snowflake exactly as I remember him. I'm glad to know his memory is still around."

"But don't you miss him?" I asked.

"Oh, yes, I do," Mr. Hooper replied. "But I haven't seen him in years. But his memory still lingers, as I'm sure he likes this old house. It's his home. I think he belongs here."

That would be cool. I kind of liked the thought of having my own special, secret pet that no one else could see.

"I can bring your pictures to you, if you want," I said.

"That would be great," Mr. Hooper said with a smile. "I brought a box with some soft padding."

"Mom and Dad went to Home Giant," I explained, "but I'll go upstairs and get them for you."

I raced into the house and retrieved the

pictures. My mind was racing from the things Mr. Hooper had told me.

So, they're not really ghosts, I thought as I went into the playroom and carefully plucked out the framed pictures. *They're only memories—memories that will be gone once I give the pictures to Mr. Hooper.*

It was still all very strange, but it made sense in a way. I was glad the mystery was solved.

I carefully carried the old pictures out to Mr. Hooper, who packed them in a box filled with white pieces of foam shaped like peanuts.

"Thank you very much," Mr. Hooper said as he climbed back into his truck. "Be sure to tell your Mom and Dad I said hello."

"I will," I said with a wave.

Mr. Hooper backed out of the driveway and drove off. I watched his truck until it vanished around a corner.

And I was glad about two things. For one, I was glad the mystery was solved. I knew what I'd seen weren't really ghosts, and the house wasn't really haunted.

And I was glad I would still see Snowflake. I was probably the only girl in the world that had an invisible cat as a pet. And no kitty litter to change!

But I had forgotten one thing:

Mr. Hooper had explained all the things that had happened in the house. He said what I'd seen were only visible memories, and I would no longer see them now that the pictures had been taken from the house.

However, that didn't explain the horrible white figure I'd seen in the yard . . . and that night, I would come face-to-face with it!

Mom and Dad came home, and I told them Mr. Hooper had stopped by. I told them he'd forgotten to take his old pictures, and I had brought them out to him. I told them he said to tell them 'hello.'

But I didn't tell them what he'd said about the house having 'memories' that only certain people could see. They would think I was making it up.

During dinner, Snowflake scampered into the kitchen. He sat right at my feet, and no one else could see him. I was glad.

And I'd forgotten all about the white figure in the backyard. I guess I thought he was gone, now that Mr. Hooper had taken the pictures from the house. I'd thought the thing I'd seen in the yard had been a memory, too.

Not true. Turns out, what I saw in the backyard was *real*.

Here's what happened:

Clay and I were in the backyard. It was long past dinner, and the sun was setting. In the summer, Mom and Dad let us stay outside after dark . . . as long as we don't leave the yard. Clay has a Frisbee that glows in the dark, and it's fun to play with.

And that's what we were doing—playing catch—when I suddenly spotted something moving near the old cemetery. Because it was dark, I could only see dark shadows . . . but something moved. Clay saw it, too.

"What was that?" he said.

I shook my head. "I don't know," I replied. "You saw it, too?"

"Yeah," Clay said. "Over by the cemetery."

While we watched, two dark silhouettes snaked

among the trees.

Who—or what—are they? I wondered. Mr. Hooper had told me all the memories were gone, now that he'd taken the pictures away.

But it was too dark to see anything but murky shadows. After a moment, we saw no more movement at all.

"I'm going inside," Clay whispered. "I'm freaked out."

He started walking, and I followed him.

Suddenly, without any warning at all, the horrible-looking white creature appeared. This time, however, he wasn't passing by like he had the night before . . . he was coming right at us!

The ghostly white figure was moving fast—much faster than it had the night before. It was moving so fast that we didn't have time to run.

"*Ahhhhhh!*" Clay screamed as the monster attacked. It bowled my brother down, and he crashed into me. We both fell to the ground in a tangled heap.

"*He got me! He got me!*" Clay squealed as he flailed about.

I rolled to the side and got to my feet. I could

feel my heart thumping in my chest.

Right in front of us, only a few feet away, the ghostly white figure hung in the air, motionless, waiting for us to make a move.

That's when I heard giggling. And laughter.

Wait a minute, I thought, and I walked up to the white creature suspended in the air. I reached out my hand and touched it.

"This isn't a ghost!" I said angrily. "This is a sheet! Someone is playing a joke on us!"

"I thought he bit me," Clay said as he got to his feet and walked to my side. He, too, reached his hand out.

Not far away, I could still hear stifled giggles and laughing.

"Whoever you are," I said, "that was *not* funny!"

"It was for *us!*" came a voice from the shadows. There was more laughter and giggling, and it sounded like it was coming closer.

"You scared the daylights out of us!" I said.

"That's what we wanted," a boy replied. "And it worked!"

A flashlight clicked on, and the beam hit me in the face.

"Hey, knock it off," I said, holding my hands up to block the bright light.

"Sorry," the boy said. He shifted the flashlight, and the beam landed on the motionless white figure hanging in the air a few feet away.

"Pretty cool, huh?" he said.

"This was all a big joke?!?!" I said.

"That's right," the boy said. "And it worked!"

In the beam of the flashlight, the 'ghost' looked cheap and cheesy, and in the daylight, it wouldn't have been scary at all. But in the dark of night, its features were blurred, and it was quite horrifying.

"We made him out of old sheets," the other boy said. It was the first time he'd spoken. "His head is only a soccer ball. We covered it with a sheet and drew his face with a permanent marker."

"Then, we ran a wire hook through the sheet," the other boy said.

"But how does it move across the yard?" Clay asked.

"We strung a fishing line from a tree in our yard to a tree way over there," he replied, pointing. "We had to climb the trees to do it, too, because we had to make it high enough so no one would run into it. All I have to do is give our ghost a push, and he moves across the yard on the fishing line."

"So, it's been *you* that I've seen around the old cemetery after dark," I said.

"Yeah," the boy said. "I saw you on the first day you moved here. I was in the cemetery."

"I thought you were my brother, and I went to the cemetery . . . but you were gone."

"I didn't want anyone to see me," the boy said, "because I was stringing up the fishing line."

"But what about the lantern I saw last night?" I asked.

"That was mine," the other boy said. "I was getting ready for bed when I remembered I left my baseball bat by the cemetery. I brought a lantern so I could see it, but I got freaked out by the shadows in the cemetery, so I ran home and left the lantern behind. I came back this morning and got it."

I was still a little mad, but I had to admit: the whole thing was pretty funny. They'd really fooled us! Clay and I really thought we were being attacked by a ghost!

"You must be the new people that moved into the old Hooper house," the boy said. "I'm Robbie, and

190

this is my neighbor, Mark."

"I'm Hannah," I said, "and this is my brother, Clay."

Just then, a woman's voice echoed through the darkness. *"Robbie! Time to come inside!"*

"I've got to go," Robbie said. "But I'll come back in the morning and show you our 'ghost' in the daylight. You might want to use it to freak out your Mom or Dad."

That was a great idea! Mom or Dad would freak out if they saw the fake ghost coming at them!

"Okay," I said.

"Yeah," Clay said. "Now that I know it's fake, I'm not scared. Actually, it's kind of cool."

"See you later," Robbie said. He reached out, pulled the fake ghost down, and unhooked it from the fishing line. He handed it to Mark, and the two boys trundled off, following the beam of the flashlight.

"We've got to use that fake ghost to scare Mom and Dad!" Clay said as we started walking back to the house.

"Yeah," I replied. "It's cool how they rigged that up. Robbie is pretty smart."

We went inside. Clay watched television, and I

went to bed early to read a book. It was about huge sea creatures in South Carolina, and it was pretty scary.

And just before I turned off the light, Snowflake wandered into my bedroom.

"There you are," I whispered as the cat leapt onto my bed. He curled up next to me, and I thought again about how cool it was that no one else could see him.

I turned off the light and thought about the book I was reading. It was scary, but I knew it wasn't true. Sea creatures like that aren't real.

At least, that's what I *thought* as I drifted off to sleep. In the morning, however, I would find out differently. Sea creatures—giant, underwater monsters—really *do* exist.

The next morning when I went outside, I saw Robbie in his backyard. He waved, and I waved back as I walked over to him.

"Hi," I said.

"Hi, Hannah," he replied. It was nice to actually be able to see what he looked like. Last night, it had been too dark.

"Where is your fake ghost?" I asked.

Robbie frowned. "I kind of got in a little bit of

trouble," he replied sheepishly. "When I went into our house last night, Mom saw what I had done. I thought I had used an old sheet, but it turns out it was one of her new ones. She was really mad. Right now, she's soaking it in the sink, trying to get the permanent marker to come off. If it won't come out, I have to buy a new sheet from my own money."

"That's a bummer," I said.

"It sure is," Robbie replied. "I don't have a lot of money."

We talked about things he liked to do and things I liked to do. I told him all about our old house and my old friends. I told him I hoped to make new friends here.

"Oh, you won't have any trouble doing that," Robbie said. "There are lots of kids around. You met Mark last night. He's great. He's one of my best friends."

"How long have you lived here?" I asked him.

"Only about a year," he said.

"Have . . . have you ever seen anything strange happen around our house?"

Robbie thought about it. "No," he said. "Nothing I can think of. The old cemetery was a little spooky when I first moved here, but, after a while, I realized there was nothing to be afraid of. Now, at my old home in Mississippi? *That's* where there's something to be afraid of."

"What?" I asked.

"Well, it's not really in my home. It's in the water. In Ross Barnett Reservoir. It's a huge lake not far from where I used to live."

"What's to be afraid of?" I asked.

"You wouldn't believe me in a million years," Robbie said. "Oh, I know it's true, because it happened to me and my friends. But when I tell people, they don't believe me."

"But what's in the lake?" I asked again. "What is there to be afraid of?"

"A giant, prehistoric shark," Robbie said.

And he was right. I wasn't sure if I believed him.

"A giant, prehistoric shark?" I said. "There's no such thing."

Robbie nodded. "Yes, there is," he continued. "It's called a Megalodon. Everyone thought they were extinct. And besides . . . they weren't supposed to live in fresh water. But this one did. I'll tell you about it if you promise not to laugh."

I thought about the book I was reading. Maybe Robbie was making the whole thing up, just like that guy who wrote the book I was reading about monster sea creatures in South Carolina.

I smiled. "Well, I can't promise I'll believe you, but I promise I won't laugh."

"Fair enough," Robbie said, and I listened as he told me his story . . . about the Mississippi Megalodon.

Next:

AMERICAN CHILLERS

AMERICA'S #1 SERIES FOR MAXIMUM CHILLS!

#25: Mississippi Megalodon

Continue on for a FREE preview!

1

Megalodon.

When I first saw the word, I didn't know what it meant. I didn't even know how to pronounce it.

Now, of course, I know *exactly* what a megalodon is. So do my friends, Tara and Landon. They know all too well what a megalodon is, and what it can do. They know, because they were with me. They saw it, too.

You see, a megalodon is a giant, prehistoric shark. At school last year, my teacher, Mrs. Biltmore, gave each of us a word to research. We had to find out what the word was, and write a five page report. When she gave me the word *megalodon* on a small piece of paper, I looked at it and frowned.

"What's a mega . . . mega . . . however you say it?" I asked her.

Mrs. Biltmore smiled at me. "You'll have to find out yourself," she said.

Great, I thought. *Whatever it is, it's probably not something cool.* I was really jealous of some of my classmates who'd been given their assignments. One was given the word 'velociraptor,' which is a fierce, meat-eating dinosaur. In fact, I had just finished reading a book about velociraptors in West Virginia. It was really freaky book. I wished I'd been given that word to research.

But, when I found out what a megalodon actually was, I was really excited. You see, a megalodon is a giant, prehistoric shark that grew to over sixty feet long!

Once I began my research, I couldn't stop. Normally, I don't really like homework. But this assignment was super cool! I worked on my assignment for a couple of hours every night. Even on weekends.

The word megalodon means 'big tooth.' Megalodons are said to have lived millions of years ago, and believed to be the largest shark that ever existed. Megalodons were so big that some scientist think they may have eaten huge whales!

I found out a lot more information about megalodons on the Internet, and even a few pictures of fossilized teeth, some of which are the size of a football.

Most scientists, however, say megalodons vanished a long, long time ago. But, there are a few scientists and researchers who believe that megalodons still exist today, in the deepest parts of the ocean.

Both groups of scientists are wrong. Megalodons *do* exist today . . . but not in the great depths of the ocean.

Megalodons—one of them, at least—live in the dark, murky depths of Sardis Lake, Mississippi, which is where I used to live.

How do I know megalodons exist? I know this, because Tara, Landon, and I came face-to-face with the gigantic beast one horrifying day last summer . . . .

ABOUT THE AUTHOR

Johnathan Rand is the author of more than 50 books, with well over 2 million copies in print. Series include **AMERICAN CHILLERS, MICHIGAN CHILLERS, FREDDIE FERNORTNER, FEARLESS FIRST GRADER,** and **THE ADVENTURE CLUB.** He's also co-authored a novel for teens (with Christopher Knight) entitled **PANDEMIA**. When not traveling, Rand lives in northern Michigan with his wife and two dogs. He is also the only author in the world to have a store that sells only his works: **CHILLERMANIA!** is located in Indian River, Michigan. Johnathan Rand is not always at the store, but he has been known to drop by frequently. Find out more at:

www.americanchillers.com

Johnathan Rand travels internationally for school visits and book signings! For booking information, call:

1 (231) 238-0338!

www.americanchillers.com